A Christmas Love Story

Sarah Baker

Published by Bright Minds Books, 2024.

This is a work of fiction. Similarities to real people, places, or events are entirely coincidental.

A CHRISTMAS LOVE STORY

First edition. October 8, 2024.

ISBN: 979-8227843753

Written by Sarah Baker.

Table of Contents

Description

Enzo and Maria's story begins with a chance encounter on Christmas Eve while shopping at a crowded mall.

Drawn to each other from the start, they quickly form an unbreakable bond that blossoms into love as they spend the holiday season together. From cozy days indoors to magical New Year's Eve moments, their relationship grows stronger with every shared experience. But it's not just the magic of Christmas that brings them together—it's the depth of their connection and the promise of a future filled with love.

A Christmas Love Story is a heartfelt tale of romance, fate, and forever.

Dedication

To everyone who believes in the magic of love, the power of chance encounters, and the beauty of new beginnings. This story is for the romantics at heart, who see the wonder in everyday moments and the possibility in every passing glance.

May you always find the love that fills your heart with warmth and the moments that take your breath away.

Preface

There's something undeniably magical about the holiday season—a time when the world seems to slow down, and love feels just a little bit stronger.

For Enzo and Maria, Christmas wasn't just about the festive lights, the snow, or the presents under the tree. It was the moment their paths crossed and their lives were forever changed. This story was born from the idea that love can be found in the most unexpected places, that fate has a way of bringing people together when they least expect it.

As you turn the pages, I hope you feel the warmth of their journey and the magic of their love.

Chapter 1: The Mall Encounter

The Christmas rush was in full swing, and the mall was a cacophony of sound—children's laughter, Christmas music blaring from every store, and the general hum of shoppers trying to get their last-minute gifts. Enzo hadn't intended to wait this long, but between work and everything else, the days had slipped by faster than he'd anticipated. Now, here he was, weaving his way through the crowded mall, hoping to find something—anything—that would be perfect for his niece, Sophia.

He found himself in the toy section of a large department store, scanning the shelves for something that wasn't a doll, since Sophia wasn't the "doll" type. His eyes landed on a colorful art set, something that she could use to explore her creative side. Just as he reached for it, his hand brushed against someone else's, and they both pulled back with a start.

"I'm sorry!" a woman's voice rang out at the same moment Enzo said the same.

Their eyes met, and for a moment, Enzo was stunned. The woman standing next to him had a warmth in her eyes that contrasted the winter chill outside. Her dark brown hair framed her face, and her cheeks were flushed, whether from the cold or from the bustling mall, he couldn't tell. She smiled, and Enzo felt the noise of the mall fade into the background.

"No, I'm sorry," Enzo said, a slight laugh escaping his lips. "Looks like we both had the same idea."

She glanced at the art set still sitting on the shelf. "I guess we both know a creative little girl," she said, her tone playful.

Enzo chuckled, grateful that she seemed as amused by the situation as he was. "My niece is eight and wants to be an artist when she grows up. What about you?"

"My little cousin," she replied. "She's nine, and she's obsessed with painting right now. I figured this would keep her busy for a while."

They both reached for the set again, but this time, they paused, realizing the humor of the situation. Enzo felt the awkward tension dissolve into something lighter. It wasn't every day he found himself chatting with a stranger while Christmas shopping, let alone one who seemed so easy to talk to.

"Well, you saw it first," Enzo said, taking a step back. "I can always find something else."

"No, no!" she insisted, shaking her head. "There's plenty of other options. I'll find something different." She flashed him another smile, this one more genuine and open, like they were old friends. "It's really no big deal."

"I feel like we're in a cheesy Christmas movie right now," Enzo joked, and to his surprise, she laughed.

"Isn't that how all the holiday romances start?" she quipped, her eyes twinkling with amusement.

Enzo smiled, feeling more at ease than he had since he'd stepped into the crowded mall. There was something about her energy that made the chaos of the holiday season feel almost bearable. She was warm, witty, and her laughter was contagious.

"I'm Enzo, by the way," he said, extending his hand, unsure why he suddenly felt compelled to introduce himself to this stranger.

"Maria," she replied, taking his hand in a firm, but soft grip. "Nice to meet you, Enzo."

There was a brief pause where neither of them seemed to know what to say next, but neither was in a hurry to leave either. The noise of the mall returned, but it felt distant, like they were in their own little bubble.

"So, Maria, are you here doing all your Christmas shopping at the last minute too, or is it just me?" Enzo asked, breaking the silence with another lighthearted comment.

Maria rolled her eyes playfully. "Last minute, of course. I always tell myself I'm going to be more prepared next year, but somehow, I end up here every Christmas Eve, frantically searching for the perfect gifts."

Enzo nodded. "Same here. I don't know how it happens. One minute it's Thanksgiving, and the next thing I know, I'm scrambling through a crowded mall like it's some sort of survival challenge."

They both laughed, and Enzo noticed how easy it was to talk to her. It felt natural, like they'd known each other longer than just a few minutes. He was already contemplating how he could extend the conversation, not ready to let her walk away yet.

"Well," Maria said, glancing down at her watch, "I should probably keep moving. I've still got a few more gifts to buy before everything closes."

Enzo felt a pang of disappointment but quickly pushed it aside. He didn't want to seem too eager, even though something about Maria intrigued him. She was different—there was a warmth and charm about her that he didn't often find.

"I understand. Christmas Eve waits for no one," Enzo said, giving a playful shrug. "But, uh, maybe we could grab a coffee or something after? I mean, if you're not too busy."

For a moment, he wondered if he'd overstepped. He hardly knew this woman, and it wasn't like him to ask a stranger out so casually. But Maria's smile didn't falter, and she looked thoughtful for a second before replying.

"You know what? That actually sounds really nice," Maria said. "There's a coffee shop down by the east entrance. How about we meet there once we've both finished?"

Enzo grinned, feeling an unexpected excitement at the prospect of spending more time with her. "Sounds perfect. I'll see you there."

As they parted ways, Enzo couldn't help but glance back over his shoulder, watching as Maria disappeared into the crowd. It was funny how fate worked sometimes. He hadn't expected much more than a stressful afternoon of shopping, but now, he had something to look forward to—someone, even.

With a spring in his step that hadn't been there before, Enzo picked up the art set and headed to the checkout. His mind was already replaying their conversation, and he couldn't help but feel like this chance encounter might just be the start of something special.

After all, it wasn't every day that you met someone like Maria—someone who made the chaos of Christmas Eve feel like a perfectly orchestrated moment of fate.

As Enzo left the store, the warmth of the holiday season finally settled in his chest, not from the festive decorations or the carols playing in the background, but from the possibility of where this day might lead.

Chapter 2: Coffee and Connection

The mall's hustle and bustle continued unabated, but Enzo was moving with a new purpose as he headed toward the coffee shop Maria had suggested. He had spent the last hour crossing items off his shopping list, but his mind kept drifting back to her. He couldn't remember the last time he felt this kind of excitement over a simple conversation. His heart beat a little faster as he approached the café near the east entrance. Through the glass doors, he spotted her already inside, sitting by a window, her hands wrapped around a steaming cup of coffee.

Maria looked up just as he entered, a smile crossing her face when their eyes met. Enzo's earlier nervousness melted away in the warmth of her gaze. He ordered his coffee and made his way to her table, feeling like this meeting was no longer by chance—it felt like it was meant to happen.

"That was quick," Maria said as he slid into the seat across from her. "Did you manage to get everything done?"

Enzo chuckled, taking a sip of his coffee before answering. "Mostly. I feel like I'm forgetting something, but I always do. How about you? Did you find the perfect gift for your cousin?"

Maria smiled, holding up a small bag at her side. "I did. I ended up getting her a painting set like I planned, just a different one. The toy store was packed, but somehow, I survived."

Enzo grinned. "You're brave. I barely made it through the crowd in one piece."

There was an ease between them, a sense that this wasn't just small talk. The conversation flowed naturally, and Enzo found himself drawn in by the way Maria spoke, how her voice carried a subtle joy that made him want to keep listening. They began exchanging stories about their holiday traditions and families. Maria explained that she was the oldest of three siblings and that Christmas at her parents' house was always a boisterous affair, with everyone pitching in to cook, decorate, and fill the house with laughter.

"And you?" Maria asked, her curiosity evident. "What's Christmas like for you?"

Enzo smiled, his thoughts turning to his family. "It's a bit quieter these days. My parents are still around, and I have an older brother who lives nearby. We usually spend Christmas Eve together at my parents' place. My niece, Sophia—she's the one I was shopping for—is the star of the show now. We all spoil her, probably a little too much."

"Sounds nice," Maria said, her eyes softening. "Christmas is such a family thing, isn't it? I can't imagine spending it any other way."

Enzo nodded. "Yeah, it's always been about family for me. I think that's why I love it so much, even with all the craziness leading up to it. It's the one time of year when everyone stops what they're doing and just comes together."

For a moment, the two sat in comfortable silence, sipping their coffee and watching the flurry of shoppers pass by the window. Enzo realized that he hadn't felt this relaxed in a long time—there was something about Maria that put him at ease, like they'd known each other far longer than just an hour or two.

"So, what do you do when you're not navigating Christmas crowds?" Maria asked, leaning forward slightly. "I'm guessing you're not a professional holiday shopper."

Enzo laughed. "Definitely not. I work as a project manager for a software company. It's not as exciting as it sounds, but it keeps me busy. What about you?"

"I'm a graphic designer," Maria replied. "Mostly freelance work. I've always been into art, and I guess I found a way to make a living out of it. It's nice because I get to choose my projects, but sometimes it can be a little isolating, you know?"

"That sounds amazing, though," Enzo said, genuinely impressed. "You get to be creative and work on your own terms. I wish I had more freedom like that in my job."

Maria smiled, though there was a hint of something deeper behind her eyes. "It has its ups and downs, like any job, I guess. But I do love what I do. It's just that sometimes, especially around the holidays, it can feel a little lonely. When you work from home, you don't have coworkers to chat with or office parties to go to."

"I get that," Enzo said, his tone softening. "The holidays can be hard in that way. Even when you're surrounded by people, it's easy to feel disconnected."

Maria looked at him for a moment, as if trying to decide how much to share. "Yeah. I guess this year's been a bit tougher for me than usual. I went through a breakup a few months ago, and I wasn't really looking forward to Christmas this year. I mean, I love my family, but it's hard not to feel like something's missing, you know?"

Enzo felt a pang of empathy. "I'm sorry to hear that," he said sincerely. "I can't imagine how tough that must be, especially around this time of year."

Maria shrugged, though her eyes flickered with vulnerability. "It's okay. I'm getting through it, and spending time with family helps. But yeah, I wasn't really expecting much from this Christmas. It's funny how things turn out, though."

Enzo's curiosity piqued. "What do you mean?"

Maria smiled, and this time it reached her eyes, lighting them up. "Well, if you'd told me this morning that I'd be sitting here having coffee with a stranger I met while fighting over a Christmas present, I probably wouldn't have believed you."

Enzo chuckled. "Yeah, it's not exactly how I planned my day either, but I'm glad it worked out this way."

Their eyes met across the table, and for a moment, the noise and chaos of the mall faded into the background. There was something between them, something unspoken but undeniable. Enzo wasn't sure what it was, but he knew he didn't want the afternoon to end just yet.

"Listen," he said, breaking the silence. "I know it's Christmas Eve and you probably have a million things to do, but would you want to keep hanging out for a bit? I mean, if you're not sick of me yet."

Maria laughed softly. "Not at all. What did you have in mind?"

Enzo thought for a moment, then his face lit up with an idea. "How about we go check out the Christmas lights downtown? They've got this huge tree set up in the square, and the lights are supposed to be amazing. We could walk around for a bit, take it easy."

Maria's smile grew. "That sounds perfect."

Enzo felt a warmth spread through him that had nothing to do with the coffee. As they stood to leave the café, he couldn't help but feel like this Christmas was shaping up to be far more special than he'd ever anticipated.

Maybe it was the magic of the season, or maybe it was something more. But whatever it was, Enzo was grateful to be sharing it with Maria.

As they walked toward the exit, side by side, Enzo realized he didn't care how crowded or chaotic the mall was anymore. This Christmas Eve, he had found something—someone—he hadn't been expecting. And suddenly, everything felt right..

Chapter 3: The Christmas Lights Walk

The crisp evening air greeted Enzo and Maria as they stepped out of the bustling mall. The sun had set, leaving the city illuminated by the soft glow of streetlights and Christmas decorations. A blanket of fresh snow covered the sidewalks, muffling the usual sounds of the city and adding a touch of quiet magic to the night. Maria wrapped her scarf more tightly around her neck, her breath forming small clouds in the cold air.

"The lights should be just a few blocks from here," Enzo said, gesturing toward the main square. His voice sounded casual, but inside, he was anything but. He hadn't planned on meeting someone like Maria today, hadn't planned on this strange but undeniable connection that seemed to form between them. But here they were, walking side by side, the evening air filling the gaps between their conversations.

"It's been a while since I've done something like this," Maria admitted as they strolled along the sidewalk. "Every year, I tell myself I'll come down to see the lights, but something always comes up."

"Well, tonight's your chance," Enzo said with a smile. "It's kind of a tradition for me. Every Christmas Eve, after all the craziness, I like to take a walk through the city. Something about the lights and the cold air just makes everything feel...calmer."

"I think I could use a little calm," Maria said, a wistful tone in her voice. She stuffed her hands into her coat pockets, her eyes scanning the snow-covered streets and festive decorations. "This year's been anything but that."

Enzo nodded but didn't press her for details. He could sense that the breakup she'd mentioned earlier had affected her more than she was letting on, and he didn't want to spoil the lightheartedness of the evening. Instead, he steered the conversation to something simpler, something that would keep them both in the present.

"You ever been to this part of the city before?" he asked, glancing over at her.

Maria shook her head. "Not really. I'm usually stuck on the other side of town with work and everything. I didn't realize how beautiful this area could be, especially at night."

They turned a corner, and the square came into view. The large Christmas tree in the center glowed with thousands of lights, casting a warm, golden hue over the surrounding area. Strings of lights hung between buildings, and various stalls lined the street, selling everything from hot cocoa to handmade ornaments. Families and couples wandered around, some taking photos, others holding hands as they admired the festive display.

"Wow," Maria said softly. "It's beautiful."

Enzo felt a small swell of pride, even though he had nothing to do with setting up the display. "Told you it was worth it."

They walked toward the tree, the large, towering symbol of the season drawing their gaze. Its ornaments sparkled in the lights, and its star shone brightly at the top. Enzo watched Maria's face as she took it all in, her eyes wide with wonder, like she was seeing Christmas through new eyes.

"I've always loved Christmas lights," Maria said after a while. "When I was little, my dad used to take me and my siblings out to see them. We'd drive around for hours, looking at all the houses. It was always my favorite part of the holidays."

Enzo smiled, imagining a younger Maria bundled up in the backseat of her dad's car, her eyes filled with the same childlike wonder. "Sounds like a great tradition."

"Yeah," Maria replied, her voice softer now. "Things changed after I got older, though. It's funny how you start to lose some of that magic when you're an adult."

Enzo nodded, understanding all too well. "I know what you mean. I think that's why I like coming here every year. It reminds me of that feeling I had when I was a kid—the excitement, the wonder. It's like, for a few minutes, I can feel it again."

They stood at the base of the tree for a while, watching as families gathered around to take pictures and children darted around in the snow. The soft hum of Christmas music from a nearby stall blended with the murmured conversations of passersby, creating a peaceful backdrop to the scene.

After a moment, Enzo noticed Maria shivering slightly in the cold. Without thinking, he slipped off his gloves and handed them to her. "Here, you look like you could use these more than I do."

Maria hesitated, then smiled gratefully. "Are you sure? I don't want you to freeze."

"I'll be fine," Enzo assured her with a grin. "Besides, I'm from a long line of cold-resistant Italians."

She laughed, accepting the gloves and slipping them on. "Thanks. I didn't realize how cold it was getting."

They resumed walking, taking their time as they moved through the square. A nearby vendor was selling hot chocolate, and Enzo suggested they get some to warm up. Soon, they were standing by a small bench, steaming cups in hand, watching the lights twinkle above them.

"So," Maria said, blowing on her hot chocolate before taking a sip, "what's your favorite part of Christmas? Aside from the lights, I mean."

Enzo thought for a moment, his gaze fixed on the tree. "I think it's the little things. The traditions. Like decorating the tree with my family or watching Christmas movies with my niece. It's not the big gifts or the parties; it's those quiet moments that make the holiday special."

Maria nodded, her expression thoughtful. "I think I miss that the most—the small moments. Life's been so busy lately that I haven't had much time to just...stop and enjoy it."

Enzo glanced over at her, catching the hint of sadness in her tone. "Maybe that's what this year is for. Maybe it's about finding those small moments again."

Maria smiled, her eyes meeting his. "Maybe."

They stood there in the glow of the Christmas lights, the world around them fading into the background once again. Enzo wasn't sure what it was about this night or about Maria that felt different, but he didn't want the feeling to end. There was something so simple, yet so profound, about standing here with her, sharing this quiet moment in the middle of the bustling city.

"You know," Maria said after a long pause, "I wasn't really looking forward to Christmas this year. But tonight...I don't know, it feels like things are starting to look up."

Enzo felt a warmth in his chest, and he smiled at her. "I'm glad to hear that."

They lingered there a while longer, neither in a rush to leave. The world outside seemed distant, and for the first time in a long time, Enzo felt like he was exactly where he was supposed to be.

After a while, Maria glanced at her phone. "I should probably head home soon. My family's expecting me for dinner."

Enzo nodded, though he felt a small pang of disappointment. "Yeah, I should probably get back, too. But, uh, I had a really great time tonight."

"Me too," Maria said softly. "Thanks for this. I didn't realize how much I needed it."

Enzo smiled. "Maybe we can do it again sometime?"

Maria hesitated for a moment, then her smile grew wider. "I'd like that."

They exchanged numbers before saying their goodbyes. As Enzo watched Maria walk away, her figure disappearing into the softly falling snow, he felt a sense of quiet contentment settle over him.

Christmas Eve had brought him something unexpected, something more than just the usual rush of shopping and family traditions. It had brought him Maria—and, perhaps, something much more than that.

Chapter 4: Ice Skating Adventures

The cold air nipped at Enzo's cheeks as he checked his phone, scrolling through a text from Maria. She had agreed to meet him at the city's outdoor ice rink, a place that had become a winter tradition for locals and visitors alike. His breath misted in the air, but the excitement of seeing her again warmed him from the inside out.

The past couple of days since their Christmas Eve encounter had felt like a dream. They'd texted back and forth, exchanging stories and jokes, and now, on Christmas morning, they were about to spend the day together. Enzo hadn't expected his holiday season to take such an unexpected turn, but he wasn't complaining. Maria was different—funny, kind, and just so easy to be around.

As he reached the ice rink, a few families were already skating in circles, children laughing as they slid unsteadily across the ice. The rink was framed by strings of twinkling Christmas lights, giving the entire place a soft, magical glow. In the distance, Enzo spotted Maria approaching, bundled up in a winter coat and scarf, her cheeks flushed from the cold.

"There you are!" Enzo called out, waving to her.

Maria waved back, her smile brightening her face. "Sorry, I'm a little late! Traffic was crazy around my place."

"No worries," Enzo said as she walked up to him. "You're just in time for me to embarrass myself on the ice."

Maria laughed, her eyes sparkling with amusement. "I should warn you—I'm not much better. It's been years since I've gone skating."

"Well, we'll be a pair of ice-skating disasters then," Enzo joked, feeling a rush of excitement at the idea of spending the afternoon with her. "Are you ready to hit the ice?"

Maria raised an eyebrow. "I guess I don't have a choice now, do I?"

They both laced up their rental skates, and Enzo helped Maria onto the ice, their hands gripping the barrier as they shuffled forward.

14

The cold air and the slippery surface beneath their feet immediately reminded them both of how long it had been since they'd last skated.

"Okay, this is a lot harder than I remember," Maria said, laughing nervously as she took an unsteady step.

Enzo grinned. "You're doing great! Look, we haven't fallen yet. That's a win."

They wobbled their way onto the ice, clutching each other for balance, laughing as they went. Maria's hand was warm in his, and Enzo was hyper-aware of the closeness between them. It felt natural, like they'd done this a hundred times before, though they both knew that wasn't the case.

The first few laps around the rink were slow and cautious, with both of them clinging to the sides for stability. Every time one of them slipped or wobbled, they burst into laughter, their playful banter filling the air.

"At this rate, we'll be Olympic-level skaters in about ten years," Maria joked, clutching Enzo's arm as they slowly made their way around.

Enzo laughed, steadying her as she nearly lost her balance. "Hey, as long as we don't break any bones, I'd call this a success."

They skated—or rather, shuffled—around the rink a few more times, gradually finding their rhythm. Enzo found himself relaxing more, enjoying the feel of the ice beneath his skates and the way Maria's laughter seemed to echo around them. The initial awkwardness faded, replaced by a sense of ease and fun.

After a while, they took a break by the rink's edge, both panting slightly from the effort and laughing at themselves.

"Okay, I think I need a breather," Maria said, pulling off one of her gloves and wiping her brow. "I forgot how much work this actually is."

"Tell me about it," Enzo agreed, leaning against the barrier. "But hey, we haven't fallen once. That's got to count for something."

Maria grinned. "True, but don't jinx it. There's still time for us to go crashing down."

Enzo chuckled, looking around at the skaters who glided effortlessly by. "Next time, we'll have to work on our technique. Maybe take some lessons or something."

Maria raised an eyebrow, giving him a playful look. "Oh, there's going to be a next time, huh?"

Enzo's heart skipped a beat at her teasing tone, but he kept his expression light. "Only if you can handle it," he shot back, grinning.

She laughed, nudging him lightly with her elbow. "I think I'll survive."

They stood in comfortable silence for a few moments, watching as the sun began to dip lower in the sky, casting long shadows across the rink. The festive lights twinkled above them, and the smell of cinnamon and roasted chestnuts from nearby food stalls filled the air. Enzo couldn't help but feel a sense of contentment wash over him. This moment—standing here with Maria, surrounded by the magic of Christmas—felt like something out of a movie.

"Enzo," Maria said softly, breaking the quiet. "Thanks for inviting me out today. I didn't realize how much I needed this."

Enzo glanced at her, seeing the sincerity in her expression. "I'm glad you came. This Christmas turned out a lot better than I expected."

Maria smiled, and for a second, the world around them seemed to fade away. It was just the two of them, standing there in the midst of holiday cheer, feeling like they'd known each other for much longer than just a few days.

After their break, they decided to give the ice one more try before calling it a day. This time, they were a little more confident, gliding—albeit unsteadily—across the rink without clinging to the barriers as much.

At one point, Maria's skate caught a small groove in the ice, and she stumbled forward. Instinctively, Enzo reached out, catching her before she could fall. The sudden closeness between them made his heart race. Maria looked up at him, her face inches from his, and for a moment, time seemed to stand still.

"You okay?" Enzo asked, his voice quieter now, the playful banter giving way to something more serious.

Maria nodded, her breath visible in the cold air. "Yeah. Thanks for catching me."

Their eyes held for a beat longer than normal, and Enzo felt an urge to close the distance between them. But before he could act on it, Maria straightened up and laughed, breaking the moment.

"Guess I spoke too soon about not falling," she said, shaking her head.

Enzo chuckled, letting out a breath he didn't realize he'd been holding. "Hey, at least you didn't hit the ice. That's progress."

They skated a few more laps, the lightness returning to their conversation, but the memory of that brief moment lingered in the back of Enzo's mind. There was something between them—something that went beyond just casual conversation and shared laughs. He wasn't sure what it was yet, but he was willing to find out.

By the time they finally left the ice rink, the sky had turned a deep indigo, and the stars had begun to appear overhead. They returned their skates and wandered toward a nearby food stall selling hot chocolate. With steaming cups in hand, they found a bench near the edge of the rink and sat down to watch the remaining skaters glide by.

"This has been fun," Maria said after a moment, blowing on her hot chocolate before taking a sip. "I'm really glad we did this."

"Me too," Enzo replied, feeling the warmth of the drink spread through him. "It's been one of the best Christmases I've had in a while."

They sat in comfortable silence for a while longer, sipping their hot chocolate and enjoying the view. The rink was beginning to empty out, and the city around them seemed to quiet as the day came to an end.

As they watched the final few skaters, Enzo felt a sense of peace settle over him. There was no rush, no pressure—just the simple joy of spending time with someone who made him feel like this Christmas was about more than just presents and traditions.

Chapter 5: Warmth in the Cold

The air was crisp, and their breath misted in front of them, but neither seemed to mind the cold. Enzo could feel the warmth of Maria's presence beside him, and the chill in the air only seemed to enhance the closeness they shared. The day had unfolded in a way he never anticipated. Christmas was always about family for him, but this year, something had shifted. He felt drawn to Maria, as if she were becoming part of his holiday story in a way that felt both unexpected and comforting.

As they approached the park, Enzo noticed a café nestled at the corner, its windows glowing with a golden light. The smell of roasting chestnuts and cinnamon wafted through the air, and through the fogged windows, he could see a few people sitting by the fireplace inside, warming themselves after a long, cold day.

"How about we go in there?" Enzo suggested, pointing toward the cozy café. "Looks like the perfect spot to warm up."

Maria glanced toward the café and nodded with a smile. "That sounds amazing. My toes are starting to feel like icicles."

They made their way inside, greeted by the immediate warmth and scent of baked goods and coffee. The walls were adorned with rustic holiday decorations—garlands of pine and holly hung around the windows, and a small Christmas tree sat in the corner, twinkling with tiny lights. Soft instrumental Christmas music played in the background, filling the room with a calm, soothing atmosphere.

Enzo led them to a table near the fireplace, where a fire crackled in the hearth, sending out waves of comforting heat. Maria slipped off her coat and settled into her chair with a contented sigh.

"This is perfect," she said, holding her hands out toward the fire. "I could stay here forever."

Enzo smiled, watching the way the firelight danced across her face, giving her a warm, almost ethereal glow. "I'm with you on that. This place is like something out of a Christmas card."

A waiter appeared, taking their orders for coffee and pastries. As they waited for their drinks, Maria leaned back in her chair, her expression softening. She seemed more relaxed now, the tension that had lingered in her eyes earlier melting away.

"Today has been so... unexpected," Maria said, her voice quieter now, as if she were reflecting aloud. "I wasn't really looking forward to Christmas this year. But it turned out to be one of the best I've had in a long time."

Enzo raised an eyebrow, surprised by her admission. "Really? What changed?"

Maria glanced at him, her eyes meeting his for a moment before looking down at her hands, fiddling with the edge of her napkin. "I guess... I just didn't think I'd enjoy it so much. I've been going through a rough patch lately—work's been stressful, and, well, there was the breakup I mentioned. I wasn't really in the holiday spirit this year."

Enzo nodded, his chest tightening a little as he thought of how difficult that must have been for her. "I'm sorry you had to go through that. Breakups are always tough, but during the holidays? That's even harder."

Maria gave him a small, appreciative smile. "Thanks. I think I was just trying to get through the season, you know? Keep my head down, do the family thing, and wait for the new year to come."

"I get that," Enzo said, leaning forward slightly. "Sometimes the holidays can make things feel heavier, especially when life's already throwing stuff at you. But I'm really glad you agreed to hang out today. It's been fun."

"It really has," Maria agreed, her smile growing a little wider now. "I wasn't expecting to have such a good time, but... I'm glad I did. I needed this."

Their drinks arrived, and they both took a moment to enjoy the warmth of their coffee, the heat from the mugs seeping into their chilled fingers. Enzo felt a sense of quiet comfort settle over him. The café, with its soft lighting and crackling fire, created a bubble of calm around them, as if the rest of the world had been put on pause.

"So," Enzo said after a few sips of coffee, "you mentioned earlier that you're a graphic designer. What kind of projects do you usually work on?"

Maria's face lit up at the mention of her work, a spark of passion in her eyes. "Mostly freelance stuff—logos, branding for small businesses, that kind of thing. I also do some illustrations and digital art on the side. It's a mix of work and personal projects, but I love it. I've always been into art, ever since I was a kid."

"That's amazing," Enzo said, genuinely impressed. "I wish I had that kind of creativity. I'm in project management, which is way more... structured. I don't get to be creative like that."

Maria shrugged, smiling. "It has its moments, but honestly, it can get lonely sometimes. Working from home, not having that office camaraderie. It's great to have flexibility, but I miss the social aspect of a regular job."

Enzo nodded. "I can see that. I guess it's one of those things where the grass is always greener. I'd love to have more flexibility, but I also love the routine and structure my job gives me. Maybe we're both in the middle of the spectrum."

"Yeah, maybe," Maria agreed, her smile softening. "But I do love what I do. Even when it's isolating, I can't imagine doing anything else."

They continued to talk, their conversation flowing easily between them. Enzo learned more about Maria's artistic inspirations, her travels, and her love for capturing moments through her art. In turn, he shared stories about his own life—his family, his niece Sophia, and his passion for hiking and outdoor adventures. The more they talked, the more he realized how much he enjoyed hearing about her life. She had a way of telling stories that made everything seem more colorful, more vivid.

At one point, Maria paused, her gaze thoughtful as she looked at Enzo. "It's funny. We've only known each other for a few days, but it feels like we've been friends for longer."

Enzo smiled, feeling the same way. "Yeah, I've been thinking the same thing. There's just something easy about being around you."

Maria chuckled softly. "Same here. Maybe it's the Christmas magic."

"Maybe," Enzo said, though he suspected it was something more than that.

They finished their drinks, but neither seemed in a hurry to leave. The fire crackled beside them, casting a soft glow over the café, and the quiet murmur of other customers created a peaceful background hum. For a while, they sat in companionable silence, watching the flames dance in the fireplace, both content to simply be in each other's company.

Finally, Maria stretched and glanced out the window. The sky was dark now, and the snow was falling more heavily, dusting the streets in a fresh layer of white.

"It's getting late," she said, though there was no urgency in her voice. "I should probably get back soon. My family's probably wondering where I am."

"Yeah, same here," Enzo agreed, though a part of him didn't want the day to end just yet.

They stood and gathered their things, bundling up again in their coats and scarves before stepping out into the cold night. The snow fell gently around them, and for a moment, Enzo and Maria stood under the streetlights, watching the flakes drift down in the quiet of the evening.

"Thank you for today," Maria said, her voice soft. "I really needed this."

Enzo smiled, feeling the warmth of her gratitude. "I'm glad you came. It was... perfect."

They stood there for a moment longer, the night peaceful around them. And though they both knew they had to part ways, there was an unspoken understanding between them—that this wasn't the end, just the beginning of something more.

"Maybe we can do this again sometime?" Enzo asked, his voice hopeful.

Maria smiled, her eyes bright despite the cold. "I'd like that."

With that, they said their goodbyes, and Enzo watched as Maria walked down the snow-covered street, her figure slowly disappearing into the winter night. He stood there for a moment, letting the silence of the evening settle over him, feeling the warmth of the day's memories linger in his heart.

Chapter 6: Christmas Eve Mass

The days following their ice-skating adventure and cozy café time had gone by in a blur of family gatherings and holiday celebrations, but Enzo couldn't stop thinking about Maria. Even amidst the laughter and warmth of his family, his thoughts kept drifting back to their moments together—the way her smile brightened even the dullest of days, the warmth in her voice when they shared their stories, and the quiet sense of connection that seemed to deepen every time they met.

It was now Christmas Eve once again, and as the day's festivities began to wind down, Enzo found himself looking forward to seeing Maria again. They had made plans earlier in the week to meet for a special Christmas Eve mass. Maria had mentioned that it was a tradition for her family to attend the service at a beautiful old church downtown, and Enzo had eagerly agreed to join her.

It wasn't something Enzo did every year. His own family's traditions were a bit more casual—opening presents on Christmas morning, followed by a large family breakfast. But something about attending the mass with Maria felt right. It was another chance to be close to her, to share in something meaningful together. And after the whirlwind of the past few days, he found himself wanting more moments like that with her.

As Enzo made his way through the softly falling snow toward the church, he marveled at how quickly things had changed. He had gone from dreading the usual holiday rush to feeling as though this Christmas had taken on a new significance—one that revolved around Maria.

The church came into view, its towering steeple illuminated by the soft glow of streetlights and the gentle twinkling of holiday decorations. The old stone building had a timeless beauty, its stained glass windows casting colorful light onto the snow-covered ground. People were streaming inside, their footsteps crunching on the snowy path, their voices hushed as they entered the serene atmosphere of the church.

Enzo spotted Maria standing near the entrance, bundled up in her coat and scarf, her hands tucked into her pockets. She looked up as he approached, her face lighting up with a smile that immediately warmed him.

"You made it!" Maria said, her voice filled with genuine excitement.

"Of course," Enzo replied, grinning as he stepped closer. "I wouldn't miss it for the world."

Maria's eyes sparkled as she gestured toward the church. "It's been years since I've come to this service. My family usually comes, but everyone's busy this year. I'm really glad you could join me."

"Me too," Enzo said, feeling a surge of warmth at the thought that Maria had chosen to spend this moment with him. "It's a beautiful church."

"It really is," Maria agreed, glancing up at the towering façade. "There's something about Christmas Eve that makes it feel even more special."

They made their way inside, the warmth of the church instantly enveloping them. The air was filled with the scent of evergreen boughs and the soft murmur of voices. Candles flickered along the aisles, casting a gentle glow that seemed to calm the soul. The interior was even more stunning than the outside, with its high vaulted ceilings and intricate stained glass windows depicting scenes from the Nativity. A large Christmas tree stood near the altar, adorned with white lights and delicate ornaments.

Enzo and Maria found seats near the middle of the congregation, settling in as the choir's soft singing began to fill the air. The atmosphere was peaceful, serene—a stark contrast to the hustle and bustle of the holiday season outside. For the first time in a while, Enzo felt a sense of stillness wash over him, as if the noise of the world had been quieted, leaving only the calm and beauty of the moment.

As they sat side by side, Enzo couldn't help but glance at Maria out of the corner of his eye. Her gaze was fixed on the altar, her expression soft and contemplative. She looked peaceful, like she was finding solace in the familiar ritual of the mass. Enzo had always admired people who found comfort in their faith, and seeing Maria in this quiet, reflective moment only deepened his feelings for her.

The mass began, and the choir's voices rose in perfect harmony, filling the church with a sense of awe and reverence. The priest spoke of hope, love, and the miracle of the Christmas season, reminding everyone of the beauty of this time of year—a time for new beginnings, for peace, and for love. Enzo found himself listening more intently than he ever had before, his thoughts aligning with the message in ways they hadn't in the past. There was something about this Christmas, about sharing it with Maria, that made everything feel more profound.

As the service continued, Enzo and Maria exchanged occasional glances, small smiles passing between them in the candlelight. There was no need for words—the quiet connection they shared was enough. The music, the prayers, the soft glow of the candles—it all seemed to create a moment suspended in time, one that Enzo would remember for years to come.

At one point, the congregation rose to sing "Silent Night," the familiar melody echoing through the church as everyone held candles, their flames flickering gently. Enzo lit his candle from Maria's, and the two stood together, their voices mingling with the rest of the congregation in a beautiful harmony.

In that moment, with the church filled with soft candlelight and the sound of "Silent Night" carrying through the air, Enzo felt something shift inside him. This Christmas Eve wasn't just about tradition or celebration—it was about the connection he was building with Maria, the quiet moments they shared, the way her presence had turned this season into something truly special. It was a feeling he couldn't quite put into words, but he knew it was real.

As the service drew to a close, the congregation began to file out of the church, the cold night air rushing in as the doors opened. Enzo and Maria lingered for a moment, both seeming reluctant to leave the peaceful warmth of the church.

"That was beautiful," Maria said softly as they stepped outside, her breath misting in the cold air.

"It really was," Enzo agreed, glancing up at the stars now twinkling in the clear night sky. "Thank you for inviting me. I don't think I've ever had a Christmas Eve quite like this."

Maria smiled, her eyes reflecting the light from the nearby streetlamps. "I'm glad you came. It meant a lot to me to share it with you."

They stood in the quiet of the evening for a moment, neither in a rush to leave. The snow continued to fall softly around them, the world hushed and serene in the wake of the mass. Enzo felt a sense of peace settle over him, the kind that only came in moments like this—when everything felt right, when the noise of life faded away, leaving only the simple beauty of the present.

"Do you want to take a walk?" Enzo asked, his voice low, as if speaking too loudly might break the spell of the night.

Maria nodded, her smile soft and warm. "I'd love that."

They walked together through the snow-covered streets, the church bells ringing softly in the distance. The night felt magical, filled with the quiet joy of Christmas Eve and the growing connection between them. Enzo didn't know what the future held, but in that moment, with Maria by his side, he knew one thing for sure: this Christmas had already become more than he could have ever imagined.

Chapter 7: The Midnight Stroll

The church bells had just struck midnight as Enzo and Maria stepped out into the crisp, snow-covered streets, their breath visible in the cold night air. Christmas Eve had officially transitioned into Christmas Day, and the world seemed to be holding its breath in the stillness of the night. The bustling city had quieted, and the streets were now nearly deserted, except for the occasional person hurrying home or a couple strolling arm-in-arm through the falling snow.

The cold was biting, but neither Enzo nor Maria seemed to notice. There was a sense of peace between them, the kind of contentment that only came from knowing that the night wasn't quite over yet. The air was filled with the scent of pine and the occasional whiff of roasting chestnuts from a vendor closing up his stall. The lights from the Christmas decorations still twinkled above them, casting a soft, festive glow over the snowy streets.

"Do you ever wonder how Christmas can feel so busy and chaotic during the day, but at night, it's like the whole world slows down?" Maria asked, breaking the quiet as they began their walk.

Enzo glanced at her, a smile tugging at the corners of his mouth. "Yeah, it's almost like everything just... pauses. Like we finally get a chance to breathe."

Maria nodded, her hands tucked into her coat pockets to ward off the chill. "I love this time of night. When everything's quiet and calm, it's like you can finally hear yourself think."

They walked in companionable silence for a while, the only sound coming from the soft crunch of their boots on the snow. The city looked like something out of a postcard—snow gently falling, Christmas lights twinkling, and the streets hushed in the stillness of the midnight hour. The chaos of last-minute shopping, crowded streets, and holiday stress felt like a distant memory now, replaced by a sense of tranquility that wrapped around them like a warm blanket.

As they strolled through the quiet streets, they found themselves wandering back toward the city square, where the towering Christmas tree still stood, its lights casting a golden glow across the freshly fallen snow. The tree was even more beautiful at night, with no crowds or bustling shoppers to distract from its grandeur. It stood as a silent sentinel over the city, a symbol of the magic and hope of the season.

"Do you want to go see the tree again?" Enzo asked, nodding toward the square. He wasn't ready for the night to end just yet, and something about the sight of the tree in the stillness of midnight felt perfect.

Maria smiled, her eyes lighting up. "I'd love that."

They made their way toward the square, the soft glow of the Christmas lights guiding their path. As they neared the tree, Enzo felt a sense of awe wash over him, the beauty of the moment settling into his bones. There was something about Christmas at midnight, something almost magical that made everything feel more significant.

"I'm really glad we did this," Maria said, breaking the silence as they reached the base of the tree. She looked up at the twinkling lights, her face illuminated by the soft glow. "It's been a while since I've had a Christmas Eve like this."

"Me too," Enzo admitted, his voice quiet. He couldn't remember the last time he had felt so at peace, so content. "This is... different. In a good way."

Maria turned to look at him, her eyes searching his. "What do you mean?"

Enzo hesitated for a moment, unsure of how to put his feelings into words. There was something about Maria—something that made this Christmas feel like more than just another holiday. It felt like the beginning of something special, something unexpected.

"I guess I just didn't expect this Christmas to be so... meaningful," Enzo said finally, his gaze meeting hers. "I wasn't really looking for anything when we met, but now... I don't know. It feels like this Christmas has changed everything."

Maria's expression softened, and for a moment, neither of them spoke. The silence between them wasn't uncomfortable, though—if anything, it felt right. The kind of silence that comes when words aren't necessary, when everything you need to say is already understood.

"I know what you mean," Maria said quietly, her breath visible in the cold air. "I wasn't expecting much from this Christmas either. But it's been... different. Special."

They stood there for a while, gazing up at the tree, the city quiet around them. The snow continued to fall softly, covering the ground in a pristine white blanket. The world felt still, almost as if it were waiting for something—something important.

As the snowflakes landed gently on their coats and hair, Enzo felt a pull in his chest. There was something about this moment, something about the way Maria looked at him with those soft, thoughtful eyes, that made him want to reach out, to close the distance between them.

Without thinking, Enzo took a step closer to Maria, his heart beating a little faster. She didn't move away. Instead, she turned toward him fully, her gaze never leaving his. There was a tenderness in her expression that sent a warmth spreading through him, despite the cold.

"Maria," Enzo began, his voice soft but steady, "I'm really glad I bumped into you that day in the mall. This Christmas... it wouldn't have been the same without you."

Maria smiled, her eyes shining with something that Enzo couldn't quite place. "I feel the same way. I've been through a lot this year, but meeting you—it feels like everything's starting to make sense again."

Enzo felt his heart skip a beat. There was something in her words, in the way she said them, that made him feel like they were standing on the edge of something big. Something real.

He hesitated for a moment, searching her eyes for any sign of hesitation. But there was none. Instead, he saw only warmth and openness—a reflection of his own feelings.

Before he could second-guess himself, Enzo reached out and gently took Maria's hand in his. Her skin was cold from the night air, but her touch sent a spark through him, a connection that felt both new and familiar at the same time.

Maria didn't pull away. Instead, she squeezed his hand lightly, her smile growing softer. They stood there, hand in hand, beneath the towering Christmas tree, the lights casting a golden glow around them. The world seemed to fade away, leaving only the two of them and the quiet of the night.

"I don't know what's going to happen next," Enzo said softly, his voice barely above a whisper. "But I want to find out. With you."

Maria's smile widened, her eyes glistening with the same emotion Enzo felt. "Me too," she said, her voice just as quiet. "I think this is the start of something... something really special."

They stood there in the snow, the world around them frozen in time. The bells from the nearby church chimed softly in the distance, and the snow continued to fall, coating the city in a fresh layer of magic.

Chapter 8: Christmas Morning Surprise

The warmth of the sun streamed through Enzo's bedroom window, casting golden light on the snow-covered streets outside. He stirred beneath his blankets, the sound of distant bells and the occasional chirp of birds blending with the peaceful silence of Christmas morning. The world seemed to move more slowly today, as if everyone was taking a collective breath, savoring the quiet beauty of the holiday.

Enzo stretched, his body still relaxed from the night before. His mind, however, was already racing with thoughts of Maria. Their midnight stroll had left him feeling more at peace—and more excited—than he had in years. There was something about Maria, something that had turned this Christmas into the most meaningful one he could remember.

As he lay in bed, staring at the ceiling, his phone buzzed on the nightstand. He reached for it, his heart doing a small flip when he saw Maria's name flash across the screen.

Merry Christmas, Enzo! :) I hope you slept well. My family is still asleep, but I was thinking—how would you feel about having breakfast together this morning? It's a bit last minute, I know, but I thought it would be nice to start Christmas with some good company. If you're not busy, of course! Let me know.

Enzo smiled, warmth spreading through him at the thought of spending more time with her. His family wouldn't mind if he disappeared for a couple of hours. After all, Christmas morning at his parents' house was usually spent lazing around until everyone gathered for a big breakfast.

He typed out a quick reply:

Merry Christmas, Maria! Breakfast sounds perfect. I'd love to join you. Where should we meet?

He hit send, already feeling the buzz of excitement. His phone buzzed again a moment later with Maria's reply:

Great! How about that little café we saw the other day? The one near the ice rink? It's open for Christmas brunch. Meet you there in an hour?

Enzo's heart raced as he typed back a quick confirmation. He leapt out of bed, the cold air snapping him fully awake, and quickly got ready. By the time he pulled on his coat and scarf, he was already imagining how the morning might go—Maria's smile, the cozy café, and the chance to spend a little more time with her before they both got swept up in family gatherings.

As Enzo made his way toward the café, the streets were quieter than usual, the city blanketed in fresh snow from the night before. The holiday decorations still twinkled in the early morning light, casting a festive glow over the streets. He could hear the faint sound of carols coming from nearby houses as families celebrated in their own ways.

The café was just as warm and inviting as he remembered it. The soft glow from the windows beckoned him inside, and the smell of fresh coffee and pastries greeted him the moment he stepped through the door. There was a small, intimate crowd of people—some couples, a few families—gathered for Christmas brunch, their laughter and conversation adding to the cheerful atmosphere.

Enzo spotted Maria sitting at a small table near the fireplace, her face illuminated by the soft, flickering light of the fire. She looked up as he approached, her smile widening when she saw him.

"Hey, you made it!" Maria said, standing to greet him.

"Wouldn't miss it for the world," Enzo replied, unable to keep the smile off his face. He took off his coat and scarf and sat down across from her, the warmth of the fire instantly soothing him.

Maria looked radiant, her cheeks slightly flushed from the cold, and her eyes sparkling with the same joy that Enzo had seen last night. He couldn't help but feel a surge of happiness at the sight of her, as if being around her made everything feel brighter.

"I'm so glad you could come," Maria said, leaning forward slightly. "I didn't want to spend Christmas morning alone, and I thought it would be nice to share it with someone... special."

Enzo felt his chest tighten at her words, a warm sensation spreading through him. "I'm glad you asked. This is already turning out to be one of the best Christmases I've had in a long time."

Maria's smile softened, and for a moment, they simply sat there, basking in the comfortable silence, the fire crackling softly beside them. The intimacy of the moment made Enzo feel like they were in their own little world, separate from the hustle of the holiday season outside.

"So, how did the rest of your family's Christmas Eve go?" Enzo asked, breaking the quiet.

Maria chuckled softly, shaking her head. "Oh, you know, the usual chaos. My younger siblings stayed up way too late, and my parents are probably going to sleep through half of Christmas morning. But it was nice. It's funny how, no matter how crazy things get, being with family just makes it all feel right."

"I know what you mean," Enzo agreed. "It's the same with my family. My niece, Sophia, has already woken everyone up by now, I'm sure. Christmas is her favorite holiday—she gets so excited, it's contagious."

Maria smiled at the mention of his niece. "You've told me about her before. She sounds adorable."

"She is," Enzo said with a laugh. "She's the light of our family. I can't wait to see her face when she opens her presents."

Their conversation flowed naturally from there, moving easily from stories about family traditions to childhood memories. They talked about the little moments that made Christmas special—Maria's family's annual gingerbread house competition, Enzo's fondness for watching old Christmas movies with his parents, the way both of them loved the quiet magic of Christmas Eve.

As they talked, the café's staff brought out steaming cups of coffee and plates of warm croissants, cinnamon rolls, and other breakfast treats. The scent of freshly baked bread and cinnamon filled the air, mingling with the crackling fire to create the perfect Christmas morning atmosphere.

"I could get used to this," Maria said, taking a sip of her coffee. "Christmas morning brunch, a cozy café... It's perfect."

Enzo smiled, feeling a wave of contentment wash over him. "Yeah, it really is. I don't think I've ever had a Christmas quite like this one."

Maria glanced at him, her eyes soft. "Neither have I."

They ate their breakfast slowly, savoring each bite and the peacefulness of the morning. The sun began to rise higher in the sky, casting long shadows across the snow outside. Inside, the warmth of the fire and the glow of the Christmas lights created a cocoon of comfort around them.

As they finished their meal, Maria set down her fork and leaned back in her chair, a satisfied smile on her face. "This has been the perfect start to Christmas. I'm really glad we did this."

"Me too," Enzo said, his voice warm with sincerity. "It's been... special. And I'm glad I got to spend it with you."

Maria's smile grew softer, her eyes locking with his. "Me too, Enzo."

They sat there for a while longer, enjoying the last few moments of quiet before the day's festivities would pull them back into the world. Outside, the snow continued to fall gently, and the city moved at its own slow pace, as if savoring the magic of Christmas morning.

Eventually, Maria glanced at the time and sighed softly. "I should probably head back soon. My family's going to wonder where I am."

Enzo nodded, though he felt a pang of disappointment at the thought of the morning coming to an end. "Yeah, I should get back too. But I'm really glad we did this."

Maria stood, slipping on her coat and scarf. "Maybe we can do it again next year? Make it a new Christmas tradition?"

Enzo's heart lifted at the thought. "I'd love that."

As they stepped outside into the fresh snow, Maria turned to him, her eyes filled with warmth. "Merry Christmas, Enzo."

"Merry Christmas, Maria," he replied softly.

They stood there for a moment, neither of them wanting to leave just yet. But finally, Maria smiled and began to walk away, her footsteps leaving soft prints in the snow.

Chapter 9: Gift Exchange

Christmas afternoon had settled into a quiet calm by the time Enzo arrived back at his apartment. His morning with Maria had left him filled with a kind of warmth that even the thick snow falling outside couldn't cool. After a busy morning spent with family, and the festive chaos that always accompanied the holiday, it felt good to have a few quiet moments to himself.

He had just kicked off his boots and started to relax when his phone buzzed. It was a text from Maria.

Maria: *Hey! I was thinking... remember how we talked about exchanging gifts? Well, I have something for you. It's small, but I'd love to drop it off if you're free!*

Enzo grinned, his heart skipping a beat. They had joked earlier in the week about swapping small presents, but it had seemed casual at the time. Now, the idea of exchanging gifts felt like the perfect way to continue their day together. He quickly replied.

Enzo: *Of course! I actually have something for you too. Want to come by my place? It's not too far from the city center, and I'll make us some hot chocolate.*

He sent his address and, after a few minutes, Maria responded.

Maria: *Sounds great! I'll be there in about 30 minutes :)*

Enzo couldn't stop smiling. He had bought a small, thoughtful gift for her the day before, something that reminded him of one of their conversations. It wasn't much, but it was personal, and he hoped she'd appreciate the gesture. As he quickly tidied up his apartment and prepared the hot chocolate, he realized how much he was looking forward to seeing her again.

The soft knock at the door came right on time. When Enzo opened it, Maria stood there with a bright smile, bundled up in a scarf and coat, holding a small gift bag in her hand.

"Merry Christmas again!" she greeted him, her cheeks pink from the cold.

"Merry Christmas!" Enzo replied, stepping aside to let her in. "Come in, get warm. I've got hot chocolate ready."

Maria stepped inside, shaking off the snowflakes that clung to her coat and scarf. Enzo could tell she had been outside for a while—the cold air followed her in, but it was quickly replaced by the warmth of the apartment.

"This is cozy," Maria said, looking around his living room, which was softly lit by the glow of Christmas lights strung up around the windows. "You really know how to create a Christmas vibe."

Enzo smiled and handed her a steaming mug of hot chocolate. "I do what I can. It's nothing compared to what we saw in the city, but I try to keep things festive."

They both sat down on the couch, sipping their hot chocolate and chatting easily about their day so far. The conversation flowed as naturally as it always did between them, and Enzo marveled at how comfortable he felt around Maria. It was like they had known each other for far longer than just a few days.

After a few minutes, Maria set her mug down and reached for the small gift bag she had brought. She looked a little shy as she handed it to Enzo, and he could tell that the gesture meant something to her.

"I know we didn't plan anything big," Maria said, "but I saw this and thought of you. It's just something small."

Enzo took the bag, his curiosity piqued. He carefully opened it and pulled out a small leather-bound notebook, the kind that felt worn and personal, like it had a story to tell. On the cover, etched in small, simple lettering, was the word "Adventures."

Maria smiled as Enzo ran his fingers over the cover. "I remembered you telling me how much you love hiking and traveling, so I thought you could use this to keep track of all your adventures. Places you've been, places you want to go... I don't know, it just seemed like something you'd appreciate."

Enzo's heart swelled at the thoughtfulness of the gift. He flipped through the blank pages, already imagining the places he could fill it with. "Maria, this is perfect. Really. I love it. Thank you."

She beamed, looking relieved. "I'm glad you like it. I wasn't sure if it was your style."

"It's exactly my style," Enzo assured her. "And now I feel like my gift isn't nearly as thoughtful."

Maria shook her head, her eyes sparkling. "I'm sure it's perfect."

Enzo reached behind him and pulled out a small box, wrapped in simple, elegant paper. He handed it to Maria, watching her expression carefully. She unwrapped it slowly, and when she lifted the lid, her eyes widened in surprise.

Inside was a delicate silver bracelet, adorned with a small charm in the shape of a star. The charm wasn't just any star—it was a replica of the one they had admired during their midnight walk, the one that had shone above the city square, casting its golden light over them.

Maria blinked, her expression softening as she looked up at Enzo. "This is beautiful," she said, her voice barely above a whisper. "How did you...?"

Enzo smiled, feeling a little bashful. "I remembered how much you loved that Christmas star when we were walking the other night. It reminded me of you, so I thought this would be a nice way to remember that moment."

Maria was quiet for a moment, her fingers lightly tracing the charm. "I don't know what to say, Enzo. This is so thoughtful. I'll treasure it."

Enzo felt a surge of warmth at her words. There was something about seeing Maria so touched by the gift that made everything feel more real, more meaningful. The star wasn't just a symbol of their walk; it was a symbol of the connection they were building—one that had started unexpectedly but had quickly grown into something special.

Maria slipped the bracelet onto her wrist, and it fit perfectly. She held it up to admire it, her smile soft and genuine. "It's perfect," she said again, her voice filled with gratitude.

They sat there in comfortable silence for a while, the fire crackling softly in the background and the smell of hot chocolate lingering in the air. The gift exchange had felt like more than just a simple holiday tradition—it had felt like a moment of shared understanding, a moment where both of them realized just how much they meant to each other.

Enzo watched as Maria absentmindedly fiddled with the bracelet, her eyes still bright with happiness. He knew then that this wasn't just a fleeting Christmas connection. There was something real between them, something that went beyond the magic of the holiday season.

"I think we just started a new tradition," Maria said softly, breaking the silence.

Enzo chuckled, feeling that same warmth spread through him again. "I think you're right. Christmas gift exchanges are going to be hard to top after this."

Maria smiled, her eyes twinkling in the firelight. "I'm okay with that."

They sat together for a while longer, talking and laughing as the snow continued to fall outside. The world seemed to slow down around them, and for the first time in a long time, Enzo felt completely content. Christmas had brought him something unexpected—something more than just the joy of the season. It had brought him Maria.

As they shared another cup of hot chocolate, their gifts resting beside them, Enzo couldn't help but feel that this was the beginning of something truly special.

Chapter 10: Enzo's Family Christmas

The rest of Christmas Day unfolded in a haze of warmth and joy for Enzo, but his thoughts remained tethered to Maria. After their gift exchange, he had reluctantly walked her to the door, promising to see her again soon. Now, back at his parents' house, the familiar comfort of his family surrounded him—the laughter of his niece, the sound of Christmas music softly playing in the background, and the smell of his mom's cooking filling the air. But despite the festive cheer, a part of him couldn't stop replaying the moments he had shared with Maria.

He was sitting in the living room with his parents and his brother when the doorbell rang, jolting him from his thoughts. His mom, busy in the kitchen, called out, "Enzo, could you get that?"

Enzo stood up, curious. He wasn't expecting anyone, and most of the family was already there. He opened the door to find Maria standing on the porch, her cheeks rosy from the cold, holding a plate of homemade cookies.

"Merry Christmas... again," Maria said, flashing him a shy smile.

Enzo blinked in surprise but quickly stepped aside to let her in. "Maria! What are you doing here?"

"I, uh, baked these with my family, and I thought I'd drop some off," Maria said, holding up the plate. "I hope it's okay I just stopped by. I didn't want to intrude."

Enzo's heart swelled. "You're not intruding at all. Come in, please. I'd love for you to meet my family."

Maria hesitated, glancing past Enzo into the house, where the sounds of Christmas dinner preparations filled the air. "Are you sure? I don't want to interrupt your Christmas."

Enzo shook his head, stepping aside to usher her in. "Trust me, they'll love you. Come on, I'd love for you to join us."

After a moment's pause, Maria stepped inside, her hesitation melting away as the warmth of the house enveloped her. She handed

Enzo the plate of cookies, and he led her into the living room, where his family was gathered.

"Everyone, this is Maria," Enzo said, introducing her to his parents, his brother, and his niece, Sophia.

His mom was the first to react, wiping her hands on her apron and stepping forward with a wide smile. "Maria! It's so nice to meet you. Enzo's told us a lot about you."

Maria looked momentarily startled but quickly smiled, the warmth of Enzo's family already easing her nerves. "It's nice to meet you too. I hope I'm not interrupting anything."

"Not at all," Enzo's dad chimed in, standing up to shake her hand. "We were just about to sit down for dinner. You're welcome to join us if you'd like."

Maria looked at Enzo, her eyes wide with surprise. "Oh, I couldn't... I mean, I don't want to intrude on your family time."

Enzo smiled, reaching out to take her hand gently. "You're not intruding, Maria. We'd love to have you."

After a brief hesitation, Maria smiled and nodded. "Okay, thank you. I'd love to."

The warmth of his family's welcome seemed to relax her, and soon Maria was chatting easily with everyone, helping to set the table and getting to know Enzo's parents. His mom, always the gracious hostess, made sure Maria felt right at home, pulling her into the conversation and offering her food as though she had been part of the family for years.

As they gathered around the dining table, Enzo couldn't help but feel a sense of contentment wash over him. This was exactly what he had hoped for—to have Maria share in the joy of his family's Christmas traditions, to see her laugh and feel at ease among the people he loved most.

Throughout dinner, the conversation flowed effortlessly. Maria shared stories about her own family's Christmas traditions, and in return, Enzo's parents shared tales from when Enzo and his brother were kids—stories that embarrassed him, of course, but he didn't mind. Seeing Maria laugh and smile as his family teased him only made the moment sweeter.

"So, Enzo tells us you're a graphic designer?" his dad asked at one point, leaning back in his chair.

Maria nodded, smiling. "Yes, mostly freelance work. It's something I've always been passionate about."

"That's wonderful," his mom chimed in. "Creative work is so fulfilling. And you get to work on your own terms—that must be nice."

Maria nodded. "It is, though it can be a little lonely sometimes. But I love it. It's what I've always wanted to do."

Enzo's mom smiled warmly. "Well, it sounds like you've found your passion. That's a gift in itself."

Maria smiled back, and Enzo felt a surge of pride. His family had embraced her without hesitation, and it was clear that Maria felt comfortable, even though she had only just met them.

As the meal wound down, the conversation turned to lighter topics—Sophia's excitement over her new toys, plans for the rest of the evening, and favorite Christmas movies. By the time dessert was served, Maria had become fully integrated into the family dynamic, laughing and joking along with the rest of them.

"So, Maria," Enzo's mom said, glancing at him with a knowing smile, "what are your plans for the rest of the day?"

Maria hesitated, glancing at Enzo before answering. "Well, I was going to head back to my parents' house in a little bit. We have a Christmas movie marathon tradition that we do every year."

Enzo's mom smiled. "That sounds lovely. You're always welcome here if you need a break from all the family craziness."

Maria laughed, nodding. "Thank you. I'll definitely keep that in mind."

As the evening wore on, Maria eventually said her goodbyes, thanking Enzo's parents for their hospitality. Enzo walked her to the door, feeling a sense of reluctance at the thought of her leaving.

"Thank you for inviting me," Maria said softly as they stood on the porch. "Your family is wonderful."

Enzo smiled, reaching out to take her hand. "I'm glad you came. It meant a lot to me."

Maria squeezed his hand gently, her eyes warm. "It meant a lot to me too."

They stood there for a moment, the snow falling softly around them, the night air crisp and cold. Enzo didn't want her to go, but he knew she had her own family to get back to.

"Do you think we could see each other again soon?" Enzo asked, his voice hopeful.

Maria smiled, her eyes sparkling. "I'd love that."

They shared a quiet goodbye, and as Maria walked away, Enzo watched her disappear into the snowy night, his heart full. This Christmas had been more than he ever could have expected, and it wasn't just the holiday spirit that had made it special—it was Maria.

Chapter 11: The Family Christmas Games

After Maria's departure from Enzo's family gathering, the house was filled with a renewed sense of holiday spirit. Enzo's parents were still buzzing about how lovely she was, and even his brother couldn't resist teasing him about her.

"She's great, man," his brother said as they cleared the table together. "You seem really happy around her. Mom and Dad were practically planning the wedding during dessert."

Enzo laughed, brushing off the teasing, though he couldn't deny the truth in his brother's words. He felt something with Maria—something real, something that went deeper than the usual holiday fling. This Christmas had changed everything, and he was beginning to realize just how much.

"Yeah, well, let's not get ahead of ourselves," Enzo said with a grin. "But thanks, I really like her."

As they finished up in the kitchen, Enzo's niece, Sophia, came bounding into the room, her eyes bright with excitement.

"Uncle Enzo! It's time for the Christmas games!" she announced, tugging at his hand.

Every year, after Christmas dinner, the family would gather in the living room for a series of lighthearted games—everything from charades to Christmas trivia to silly physical challenges. It was a tradition that had started when Sophia was younger, but it had since become one of the highlights of the holiday, bringing out everyone's competitive spirit.

Enzo grinned and allowed himself to be pulled into the living room, where the rest of the family was already gathering. His mom had set up a small table with snacks and drinks, and the fireplace crackled warmly in the background, casting a cozy glow over the room.

"Okay, everyone," his dad announced, standing in the middle of the room with a playful grin. "You know the rules—no cheating, no whining when you lose, and most importantly, have fun!"

Sophia clapped her hands together, bouncing on her toes. "I want to start with charades! I'm really good at it!"

Enzo laughed and took a seat on the couch, watching as Sophia picked up the little box of charades cards and started handing them out. His family quickly divided into teams, with Enzo and his brother on one side and his parents and Sophia on the other.

The first round of charades went by in a blur of laughter. Sophia, determined to win, acted out her clues with over-the-top dramatics, which only made everyone laugh harder. Enzo's brother was competitive, as always, but his guessing was hilariously off, much to everyone's amusement. The room was filled with the sound of laughter and playful teasing, the warmth of the holiday games wrapping around them like a cozy blanket.

As the game continued, Enzo couldn't stop thinking about Maria. He wondered what she was doing with her family—if they had similar holiday traditions or if she was thinking about him too. Every now and then, his phone buzzed with a message from her, and he couldn't help but smile every time he saw her name pop up on the screen.

Maria: *We're just about to start our movie marathon. I'll try not to fall asleep halfway through, but no promises! Hope you're having fun with your family :)*

Enzo: *I'm in the middle of a cutthroat charades game with Sophia. Wish me luck! Enjoy the movies, and I'll talk to you soon.*

With a grin, Enzo slipped his phone back into his pocket just in time for the next round of charades. This time, it was his turn to act out the clue, and he stood up, taking the card from Sophia's hand. He glanced at it and smirked—it was a classic Christmas movie, and he had a feeling he could pull this one off.

He began acting out the scenes from "Home Alone," pantomiming the slapstick traps Kevin sets for the burglars, his family watching with amused expressions. His brother was quick to catch on, shouting out, "Home Alone! That's it!" just as Enzo mimicked the famous scream from the movie.

The room erupted in laughter, and Enzo sat back down, feeling the familiar joy of Christmas wash over him. This was what he loved most about the holiday—the shared moments, the laughter, and the simple pleasure of being with family.

As the charades game came to an end, Sophia declared herself the unofficial winner, much to everyone's amusement. She then insisted they move on to Christmas trivia, which was another family favorite. His mom pulled out a deck of trivia cards, and soon they were all competing to see who knew the most obscure facts about Christmas history, holiday songs, and traditions from around the world.

Enzo loved the playful competitiveness of it all. Even though the games were lighthearted, they brought out the best in his family, reminding him of how much these small moments mattered.

During one of the trivia rounds, Enzo's phone buzzed again. He glanced at it discreetly, not wanting to disrupt the game. It was another message from Maria, but this time it was a photo—her family sitting on the couch, wrapped in blankets, with a Christmas movie playing on the TV in the background. Maria had added a little caption:

Maria: *The Christmas movie marathon in full swing! Wish you were here to see my dad try to stay awake during "Elf."*

Enzo chuckled softly to himself, imagining the scene. He quickly typed back:

Enzo: *Looks cozy! I'd say you should come over here and join our trivia game, but I think Sophia would dominate everyone.*

He could almost hear Maria laughing as he sent the message, and the thought made him feel even closer to her, despite the distance between them at the moment. The easy connection they shared felt like something he had always been missing—like he had known her for far longer than just a few days.

The games continued late into the evening, with Enzo's family growing more animated with each round. His mom was surprisingly good at the trivia, and his dad, who normally stayed out of the competitive fray, ended up taking the lead in a physical challenge that had everyone doubled over with laughter.

By the time the games were finished, and they had crowned an unofficial family champion—Sophia, of course—the room was filled with the kind of happiness that only came from spending time with loved ones. The fire in the hearth had died down to glowing embers, and the room was cozy with the remnants of laughter still hanging in the air.

As they settled down for a late-night snack, Enzo leaned back in his chair, his thoughts drifting once again to Maria. She had become such an important part of his holiday so quickly, and he couldn't help but feel like this Christmas—these moments with his family, the games, the laughter—had all been made better by the thought of her.

Enzo's mom must have noticed the far-off look in his eyes because she smiled and nudged him playfully. "You seem distracted. Thinking about someone special?"

Enzo chuckled, not bothering to hide the truth. "Yeah, I guess I am."

His mom's smile softened. "She seems like a lovely girl, Enzo. I'm happy for you."

Enzo felt a warmth spread through him at his mom's words. "Thanks, Mom. I think she's pretty special too."

They sat in comfortable silence for a while, the sounds of the quiet house settling around them.

Chapter 12: A Walk in the Snow

Christmas Day had started to wind down, and Enzo found himself standing by the window, watching the snow fall steadily outside. The laughter from the family games earlier had faded into a peaceful silence as the evening approached. His family had retreated to their respective corners of the house—his mom was reading a book by the fire, his dad was already dozing off in his chair, and Sophia was playing quietly with her new toys in the living room. It was a perfect, cozy Christmas evening, but Enzo's thoughts were still on Maria.

The messages they had exchanged throughout the day had been lighthearted and playful, but there was something about the quiet of the evening that made him want to see her again. He had a sudden urge to share this moment with her—to go for a walk in the snow, just the two of them, away from the noise of the world, where everything was peaceful and still.

Without thinking too much, Enzo pulled out his phone and sent Maria a quick message.

Enzo: *Hey, how's the movie marathon going? If you're up for it, how about a walk in the snow? It's beautiful outside right now.*

He hit send and waited, his heart beating a little faster in anticipation. It was a long shot, given that she was probably still with her family, but he couldn't shake the feeling that tonight would be the perfect time for them to share something special.

A few minutes later, his phone buzzed with a reply.

Maria: *That sounds amazing. I could definitely use some fresh air after all this movie-watching! Meet you in 30 minutes?*

Enzo smiled, feeling that familiar warmth spread through him. He quickly replied to confirm and grabbed his coat and scarf, telling his mom he was stepping out for a bit. She gave him a knowing look, but didn't ask any questions—she could probably guess where he was headed.

The streets were quiet as Enzo made his way toward the park where he and Maria had agreed to meet. The snow had blanketed the city in a pristine layer of white, and the streetlights cast a soft glow on the snow-covered ground, making everything look magical. The festive Christmas lights still twinkled from the houses, but the streets themselves were nearly deserted, as most people were indoors with their families, enjoying the last few hours of Christmas.

When Enzo reached the park, he spotted Maria standing near the entrance, her figure silhouetted against the soft glow of the streetlights. She was bundled up in her coat and scarf, her hands tucked into her pockets, and when she saw him approaching, she smiled, her eyes lighting up in that way that made his heart race.

"Hey," Maria said as he walked up to her, her voice soft in the stillness of the night. "It's so quiet out here. I love it."

Enzo smiled, slipping his hands into his own pockets to ward off the cold. "Yeah, it's like the whole world's gone to sleep. Just us and the snow."

They started walking together, their footsteps crunching softly in the snow. The park was even more beautiful at night, with the trees dusted in white and the paths winding through the quiet, snow-covered landscape. The occasional Christmas light twinkled in the distance, adding a touch of festive warmth to the scene.

For a while, they walked in silence, the peacefulness of the night wrapping around them like a blanket. Enzo felt the weight of the day's celebrations lifting off his shoulders, replaced by a calm sense of contentment. He was here, with Maria, in a moment that felt timeless.

"I'm really glad you suggested this," Maria said after a while, glancing over at him. "It's been a great Christmas, but I needed some quiet time."

"Me too," Enzo replied, his breath visible in the cold air. "I couldn't stop thinking about you today."

Maria smiled, a soft blush creeping into her cheeks. "I was thinking about you too. My family loved the gifts you gave me. I showed them the bracelet, and they all agreed that you have excellent taste."

Enzo chuckled, his heart lifting at the thought. "I'm glad they liked it. I was nervous about what to get you."

"Well, you nailed it," Maria said, holding up her wrist to show him the bracelet glinting in the moonlight. "I haven't taken it off since you gave it to me."

They continued walking, their conversation flowing easily between them. Maria shared stories about her family's Christmas traditions, and Enzo found himself laughing along with her as she described her dad's annual attempt to stay awake through the entire movie marathon—a tradition that, apparently, always ended with him snoring halfway through the second movie.

As they reached a small clearing in the park, where the trees opened up to reveal a snow-covered meadow, Enzo paused, turning to face Maria. The soft light from the streetlamps and the glow of the snow made everything look dreamlike, and for a moment, he felt like they were the only two people in the world.

"Maria," Enzo said softly, his breath catching in his throat. "I'm really glad we met."

Maria looked up at him, her eyes filled with that same warmth he had felt from the beginning. "I am too, Enzo. I didn't expect this Christmas to be anything special, but then you came along and... well, you changed everything."

Enzo felt his heart skip a beat. There was something in her voice, in the way she was looking at him, that made him feel like this moment was more than just a simple walk in the snow. It was a turning point, the moment where everything that had been building between them became real.

He took a step closer to her, reaching out to gently take her hand in his. Maria didn't pull away. Instead, she stepped closer too, her breath mingling with his in the cold air.

"I feel the same way," Enzo said, his voice barely above a whisper. "This Christmas... it wouldn't have been the same without you."

For a moment, they stood there, the world around them silent and still. Enzo could feel his heart racing in his chest, but he wasn't nervous. This felt right—like the culmination of everything that had happened between them over the past few days.

"This has been the best Christmas I've ever had," Maria whispered, her voice soft but filled with certainty.

Enzo smiled, his heart full. "For me too."

Chapter 13: Maria's Invitation

The next morning, Enzo woke up with a smile still lingering from the night before. His walk in the snow with Maria had been more than just magical—it had been transformative.

As he got dressed, his phone buzzed on the nightstand. It was a message from Maria.

Maria: *Morning! I hope you slept well. So, my family's having a Christmas lunch today, and I was wondering if you'd like to come? No pressure, but it would be great to have you meet everyone. :)*

Enzo felt his heart leap. The idea of meeting Maria's family felt both exciting and nerve-wracking at the same time, but he didn't hesitate. He wanted to spend more time with her, and meeting her family felt like the natural next step.

Enzo: *I'd love to. What time should I come by?*

A few minutes later, her response popped up.

Maria: *Great! Come by around noon. I'll send you the address. It's pretty casual, so no need to dress fancy. My family's very laid-back. :)*

Enzo grinned as he sent his confirmation, feeling a rush of excitement. He spent the rest of the morning getting ready, making sure to pick up a small bouquet of flowers to bring along as a gesture of goodwill. He wanted to make a good impression, and while Maria had assured him that her family was laid-back, he figured it couldn't hurt to show up with something thoughtful.

As noon approached, Enzo made his way across town, the snow from the night before still fresh on the ground, but the skies had cleared to reveal a bright, crisp winter day. His heart raced a little as he followed the directions Maria had sent him, finally pulling up to a cozy-looking house with Christmas decorations adorning the front porch.

He took a deep breath, straightened his jacket, and headed up the walkway. Before he could knock, the door swung open, and Maria was there, smiling warmly.

"You made it!" she said, stepping aside to let him in.

Enzo stepped inside, handing her the flowers. "I wouldn't miss it. These are for your mom. I figured it'd be a nice way to say thanks for having me."

Maria's eyes softened as she took the bouquet. "That's so sweet, Enzo. She's going to love them. Come on, let me introduce you to everyone."

The house was filled with the smell of delicious food—roast chicken, potatoes, and freshly baked rolls—and the sounds of holiday music playing softly in the background. Maria led Enzo into the living room, where her family was gathered, chatting and laughing as they prepared for the meal.

"Everyone, this is Enzo," Maria announced, her hand resting lightly on his arm. "Enzo, this is my mom, my dad, and my younger siblings, Nick and Lucy."

Her family turned toward him, all smiles and warmth. Maria's mom, a petite woman with kind eyes, stepped forward first, taking the bouquet from Maria's hands.

"These are lovely, thank you so much," she said, giving Enzo a warm smile. "It's so nice to finally meet you. Maria's told us a lot about you."

Enzo smiled, feeling a sense of relief at the warmth of her welcome. "It's great to meet you too. I'm happy to be here."

Maria's dad, a tall man with a jovial expression, stepped forward next, shaking Enzo's hand firmly. "Good to meet you, Enzo. Anyone who makes my daughter smile this much is alright in my book."

Enzo laughed, appreciating the casual tone. "Thank you, sir. I'm really glad to be here."

Her younger siblings, Nick and Lucy, waved from the kitchen, where they were busy helping set the table, and Enzo gave them a friendly nod in return. He already felt at ease, the initial nerves melting away as Maria's family welcomed him with open arms.

"Come on, sit down," Maria's mom said, gesturing toward the dining table. "Lunch is almost ready. I hope you're hungry!"

As they settled into the dining room, the conversation flowed easily. Maria's family was just as relaxed and laid-back as she had described. Her mom and dad were full of stories—about Maria's childhood, her siblings, and their family traditions—and they didn't hold back from teasing her a little, much to Maria's amusement. Enzo found himself laughing along, already feeling like part of the group.

"You must tell us more about yourself, Enzo," Maria's mom said at one point, her eyes twinkling. "Maria's told us bits and pieces, but I'm curious to hear about your family and what you do."

Enzo smiled, glancing at Maria before replying. "Well, I grew up not far from here. My family's pretty small—just my parents, my older brother, and my niece, Sophia. I work as a project manager for a software company, though lately I've been thinking about getting back into hiking and exploring more in my free time."

Maria's dad nodded thoughtfully. "Hiking, huh? We've got some great trails around here. Maria used to love hiking when she was younger, didn't you, sweetheart?"

Maria chuckled, nodding. "Yeah, I used to go all the time with my dad. It's been a while, though. I've been meaning to get back into it."

Enzo's heart lifted at the idea of going hiking with Maria—yet another shared interest that brought them closer. He felt more at ease with every passing moment, the initial nerves gone as he realized just how natural this all felt. Maria's family was warm, funny, and clearly adored her. And seeing her in this setting—surrounded by her loved ones—only deepened Enzo's feelings for her.

The meal was filled with more laughter and conversation. Maria's mom was an excellent cook, and the food was as delicious as the company. Enzo found himself swapping stories with Nick and Lucy, who were younger but just as charming and easy to talk to as the rest of the family. By the time dessert rolled around—Maria's mom's famous apple pie—Enzo felt completely at home.

After lunch, they gathered in the living room, the cozy warmth of the fire filling the room as the holiday music played softly in the background. Maria's dad pulled out an old family photo album, and soon they were flipping through pictures of Christmases past, much to Maria's mock embarrassment.

"Oh no, not the baby pictures," Maria groaned, hiding her face as her mom pointed out a particularly adorable photo of her dressed as an angel in a childhood Christmas pageant.

Enzo laughed, nudging her playfully. "I think you make a pretty cute angel."

Maria rolled her eyes but smiled, clearly enjoying the moment despite her teasing protest.

As the afternoon wore on, Maria's family began to wind down, and Maria stood up to walk Enzo to the door. The rest of her family waved goodbye, thanking him for coming and telling him he was welcome anytime. It felt good to know that they had accepted him so easily.

Once they were outside, standing on the porch with the crisp winter air swirling around them, Maria turned to him, her eyes soft with gratitude.

"Thank you for coming today," she said quietly. "It meant a lot to me that you were here."

Enzo smiled, reaching out to take her hand. "It meant a lot to me too. Your family is wonderful."

Maria squeezed his hand gently, her eyes bright with emotion. "I'm really glad you got to meet them. And I think they like you."

Enzo chuckled. "Well, I'm glad to hear that. I like them too. And I like you."

Maria smiled, her breath visible in the cold air. "I like you too, Enzo."

They said their goodbyes, promising to see each other again soon.

Chapter 14: Christmas Caroling

Enzo had never done anything quite like this before, but when Maria invited him, he eagerly agreed. The idea of spending more time with her, especially surrounded by the warmth of her family's traditions, was irresistible.

The evening was crisp and clear, with stars twinkling in the dark sky as Enzo made his way to Maria's house. Snow still clung to the rooftops and sidewalks, but it was no longer falling, giving the city a peaceful, frozen beauty. When he arrived, he was greeted by the sound of laughter and holiday music spilling out from the front door.

Maria opened the door with a wide smile, bundled up in a cozy scarf and gloves. "You made it! Are you ready to sing?"

Enzo chuckled as he stepped inside, shaking the cold from his coat. "Well, I'm not sure you're going to want to hear me sing, but I'm ready to try."

Maria laughed, her eyes twinkling. "Don't worry, no one here is a professional. It's all about having fun."

The inside of the house was warm and inviting, with twinkling lights still wrapped around the banisters and the faint smell of gingerbread lingering in the air. A group of about fifteen people, including Maria's parents, siblings, and a few of their neighbors, were gathered in the living room, chatting and sipping hot chocolate in preparation for their evening of caroling.

Maria's mom waved at Enzo from across the room. "Enzo! It's so great to see you again. Are you ready to sing your heart out?"

Enzo smiled and waved back, feeling the familiar warmth of Maria's family's hospitality. "I'll do my best!"

Before long, the group was ready to head out, bundling up in coats, hats, and gloves to brave the cold. They gathered on the front porch, songbooks in hand, and Maria's dad gave a playful signal to start the first song. The group launched into a lively rendition of "Jingle Bells," and Enzo, standing beside Maria, couldn't help but smile as they sang together, their voices blending with the others in the frosty night air.

At first, Enzo felt a little self-conscious about his singing, but as they made their way down the street, stopping at houses along the way, his nervousness faded. The joy of the moment—of being part of something so simple and festive—washed over him. It wasn't about how well they sang; it was about the laughter and warmth that came from sharing the experience with Maria and her family.

Maria looked up at him after they finished "Deck the Halls," her cheeks pink from the cold and her breath misting in the air. "You're doing great!" she said, her smile wide and genuine.

Enzo grinned. "I'm just trying to keep up with you. You've got a great voice."

Maria laughed softly. "Thanks, but I think we all sound pretty good together. It's the Christmas magic."

As they continued caroling, Enzo noticed how much joy Maria took in the tradition. She sang with enthusiasm, her face lighting up as they moved from house to house, spreading cheer to their neighbors. Enzo could see how much this meant to her, and he felt grateful to be part of it—to share this moment with her and to feel like he was becoming part of her world.

They stopped in front of one particularly festive house, where a group of children gathered at the window to listen. The group launched into "Silent Night," and Enzo couldn't help but feel a sense of peace as they sang the familiar melody. The snow-covered street, the twinkling lights, and the soft glow of the holiday season created a perfect backdrop for the song, and Enzo felt completely in the moment.

When the song ended, the children at the window clapped, and the group smiled and waved as they moved on to the next house. Enzo glanced over at Maria, who was smiling softly, her eyes filled with contentment.

"This is one of my favorite parts of the holidays," she said quietly as they walked side by side. "I love how it brings people together. It's just… simple, you know? No stress, no rush. Just music and laughter."

Enzo nodded, understanding exactly what she meant. "It's really special. I've never done anything like this before, but I love it. I'm glad you invited me."

Maria glanced up at him, her eyes bright with emotion. "I'm glad you came. I wouldn't have wanted to do this without you."

They continued down the street, the group's voices filling the night with Christmas cheer. As the evening went on, Enzo found himself fully immersed in the experience. It didn't matter that the holidays were technically over—there was something about this night, about being with Maria, that made it feel like Christmas was still in full swing.

After a few more songs and plenty of laughter, the group circled back to Maria's house, where her mom had prepared hot cider and cookies to warm everyone up. The group gathered in the living room once again, the fire crackling in the hearth as they shared stories and relived the highlights of the caroling adventure.

Enzo sat beside Maria on the couch, their hands intertwined beneath the blankets they had pulled over their laps. The warmth of the fire and the contentment of the evening filled the room, and for a moment, it felt like time had slowed down. The sound of laughter and the crackling of the fire created a cozy backdrop, and Enzo couldn't help but feel that this was exactly where he was meant to be.

"I think you're officially part of the caroling crew now," Maria teased, nudging him playfully. "We'll have to make sure you're on the list for next year."

Enzo laughed softly, his heart full. "I'd love that. I'm starting to think I'm becoming a fan of all your family traditions."

Maria smiled, her eyes softening. "Well, you're welcome to join us for as many as you'd like."

They sat in comfortable silence for a moment, the fire casting a soft glow over the room. Enzo glanced at Maria, feeling a deep sense of gratitude for everything they had shared so far. The connection between them had grown quickly, but it felt right. It felt like the beginning of something lasting.

As the evening wound down and the guests began to trickle out, Maria's family thanked Enzo for coming, telling him once again how happy they were to have him there. Enzo felt truly welcomed—like he was becoming part of something bigger than himself.

After everyone had left, and the house had quieted down, Maria walked Enzo to the door. The night outside was still, with fresh snow falling gently around them, and the silence felt peaceful.

"Thank you for coming tonight," Maria said softly, her breath visible in the cold air. "I had such a great time."

Enzo smiled, reaching out to take her hand. "I had an amazing time too. Thank you for including me."

They stood there for a moment, the snow falling softly around them.

Maria smiled up at him, her eyes shining. "This has been the best holiday season," she whispered.

Enzo smiled, his heart full. "It really has. And it's not over yet."

Chapter 15: Late Night Reflections

That night, after the caroling, Enzo found himself back at his apartment, sitting on his couch with only the soft glow of the Christmas tree lights illuminating the room. It had been a long day—filled with music, laughter, and the warmth of Maria's family—but now, in the stillness of the night, he had time to reflect on everything that had happened over the past few weeks.

The quiet of his apartment contrasted sharply with the lively atmosphere of Maria's house earlier in the evening. Enzo sipped a cup of tea, staring out the window at the gently falling snow, and thought about how much his life had changed in such a short amount of time. When he'd first walked into that mall on Christmas Eve, he hadn't expected anything more than a rushed day of shopping. Yet now, here he was, having shared countless meaningful moments with someone who had quickly become so important to him.

Enzo set his cup down on the coffee table and leaned back on the couch, letting out a long breath. The holidays had always been a time for family, for togetherness, but this year had been different—this year, he had found Maria. And with her, he had found something that felt deeper than just a holiday romance.

He thought about their walk in the snow and how natural it had felt to be with her. The connection they shared wasn't just about the magic of Christmas—it was real, grounded in who they were as people. It was something he knew would last beyond the holiday season.

But as the excitement of their whirlwind connection settled into the quiet of the night, Enzo found himself reflecting on what the future might hold. They had shared so much already, but there was still so much more to discover. He wondered where this new relationship would take them. Would they continue to grow closer, or would the magic fade once the lights came down and the snow melted?

Enzo shook his head, dismissing the thought. He knew this wasn't just a fleeting connection. There was something about Maria that made him feel like they were building something solid, something lasting. Still, the vulnerability of falling for someone so quickly brought with it a touch of uncertainty.

His phone buzzed on the table, pulling him from his thoughts. It was a text from Maria.

Maria: *I can't stop thinking about tonight. It was so special. Thank you for being a part of it.*

Enzo smiled, his heart lifting at her words. He quickly replied.

Enzo: *It was amazing. I'm still thinking about it too. You, your family, everything—it was perfect.*

He set his phone down, feeling a sense of peace wash over him. If there was one thing he knew for sure, it was that Maria felt the same way he did. She had opened up to him, shared her world with him, and in return, he had done the same. That kind of connection didn't come around often, and he wasn't about to let it slip away.

Enzo stood up and walked over to the window, staring out at the snowy street below. The city was quiet now, with only a few cars passing by and the streetlights casting long shadows on the ground. It was the kind of night that made everything feel reflective, like the world had paused just long enough for him to catch his breath.

He thought about the first time he had seen Maria, their chance encounter at the toy store, and how their hands had brushed against each other as they reached for the same gift. It seemed like a lifetime ago now, but in reality, it had only been a matter of weeks. So much had happened in such a short span of time, and yet it all felt so natural, as if they were always meant to find each other.

There was a knock at the door, interrupting his thoughts. Enzo glanced at the clock—it was late, too late for a visitor—but he wasn't worried. He walked over to the door and opened it, surprised to find

Maria standing there, bundled up in her coat, her cheeks flushed from the cold.

"Maria?" Enzo asked, blinking in surprise. "What are you doing here? It's so late."

Maria smiled softly, her breath visible in the cold air. "I know, I'm sorry to just show up like this. But I couldn't stop thinking about tonight... about you. I didn't want to go home without seeing you again."

Enzo's heart swelled, and he stepped aside to let her in. "You don't have to apologize. I'm glad you came."

Maria stepped inside, shaking the snow from her coat, and Enzo could see the same emotions in her eyes that he had been feeling all night—uncertainty, excitement, and something deeper, something real. She glanced around his apartment, taking in the cozy atmosphere before turning back to him.

"I just... I don't know," Maria said, her voice soft but filled with emotion. "Everything has been happening so fast, and I didn't want the night to end without telling you how much you mean to me. I know it's only been a few weeks, but it feels like I've known you for so much longer."

Enzo's breath caught in his throat, and for a moment, he didn't know what to say. Her words echoed his own thoughts, and the vulnerability in her voice only made him feel more deeply for her.

"I feel the same way," Enzo said quietly, stepping closer to her. "I've been thinking about you all night. I've never felt like this before, Maria. Not this fast, not this deeply."

Maria's eyes softened, and she reached out, taking his hand in hers. "I'm just... I'm scared," she admitted. "I'm scared of how fast this is happening, but I'm also scared of not following it. It feels real, Enzo. It feels like something I don't want to lose."

Enzo squeezed her hand gently, his heart pounding in his chest. "We don't have to rush anything. But I don't want to lose this either. Whatever happens, whatever we decide to do, I want to do it together."

Maria smiled, her eyes shining with emotion. "Together."

Chapter 16: A Stroll Through the Park

The next date was in the nearby park. Enzo arrived at the park first, standing near the entrance as he waited for Maria. The park had always been one of his favorite places to clear his head, and today, with the snow blanketing the ground and the paths winding through the trees, it looked like something out of a winter wonderland. The bare branches of the trees were dusted with snow, and the lake in the center of the park was frozen over, reflecting the pale light of the winter sky.

As he stood there, his breath visible in the cold air, Enzo spotted Maria approaching, bundled up in her coat and scarf. Even from a distance, she looked radiant—her cheeks flushed pink from the cold, her eyes bright and warm as she smiled at him.

"Hey," she greeted him as she reached his side, her breath misting in the air. "I'm sorry I'm a little late. The snow slowed me down."

"No problem," Enzo said, smiling warmly as he pulled her into a hug. "You look great."

Maria laughed softly, adjusting her scarf. "Thanks. I'm really glad we decided to do this. I've been looking forward to it."

"Me too," Enzo agreed, taking her hand as they began to walk along the snow-covered path. The crunch of the snow beneath their boots was the only sound that broke the peaceful silence of the park.

They walked in comfortable silence for a while, the cold winter air refreshing against their faces as they took in the beauty of the snow-covered landscape. Despite the cold, there was something warm and cozy about being out here together, away from the bustle of the holiday season and the noise of the city.

The park was quiet, with only a few other couples and families out for a walk. The stillness allowed them to talk easily, without distractions, and Maria seemed especially relaxed as they strolled hand in hand.

"So," Maria said after a while, glancing at Enzo with a playful smile, "what's next for you now that the holidays are winding down? Do you have any big plans for the new year?"

Enzo shrugged, his gaze drifting over the snow-covered trees. "I haven't really thought about it much yet. I guess just getting back to work and figuring out what I want to do next. But honestly, after everything that's happened recently, my priorities feel like they're changing."

Maria raised an eyebrow, curious. "How so?"

Enzo smiled, squeezing her hand gently. "I guess I've realized that it's not all about work and routine. Meeting you has made me think about the kind of life I want to build—something that's more meaningful, you know? I don't want to just go through the motions."

Maria's expression softened, and she looked down at their intertwined hands. "I know what you mean. I've been thinking the same thing lately. The holidays have been so much more special because of you. It's made me realize how important it is to be present and not take things for granted."

They continued walking, their conversation turning to lighter topics—their favorite places to visit, the hobbies they wanted to pursue in the new year, and the things they still wanted to learn about each other. Enzo felt a sense of ease as they talked, as if this kind of openness and honesty was becoming the foundation of their relationship.

At one point, they reached a bench near the frozen lake, where the reflection of the snow-covered trees mirrored perfectly on the glassy surface. Enzo gestured to the bench, and they sat down, the peacefulness of the park wrapping around them.

"This park is beautiful in the winter," Maria said, her voice quiet. "I used to come here a lot when I needed to think. It's one of those places that just makes everything feel... calm."

Enzo nodded, glancing out at the frozen lake. "Yeah, it's always been a special place for me too. I come here when I need to clear my head. But today, it feels different—like everything is falling into place."

Maria smiled, leaning her head on his shoulder. "It really does."

They sat there for a while, watching as a few children skated on the lake in the distance, their laughter echoing faintly across the park. The cold didn't bother them; the warmth between them made everything feel perfect.

"You know," Maria said softly after a few moments, "I've been thinking a lot about how quickly things have moved between us. And at first, I was a little scared, but now... I'm not."

Enzo turned to look at her, his brow furrowing slightly. "What do you mean?"

Maria sat up a little straighter, her eyes meeting his. "I mean, I was scared of how fast everything was happening. It felt like we were getting closer so quickly, and I wasn't sure if I was ready for it. But now, I realize that maybe this is exactly how it was supposed to happen."

Enzo felt his heart lift at her words. He had been thinking the same thing, but hearing her say it made everything feel even more real. "I feel the same way," he said quietly. "I wasn't expecting any of this when we met, but now, I can't imagine things going any other way."

Maria smiled, her eyes bright with emotion. "I guess what I'm trying to say is... I'm all in, Enzo. I want to see where this takes us. I'm not scared anymore."

Enzo felt a surge of emotion as he looked at her, his heart swelling with gratitude and affection. He reached out, taking both of her hands in his. "I'm all in too, Maria. Whatever happens, I want to face it with you."

For a moment, they simply sat there, holding hands, the weight of their words settling between them. It was a promise—a commitment to whatever lay ahead.

Chapter 17: A Cozy Day Indoors

The cold winter weather seemed to settle in even more as January rolled on, and with it came the perfect excuse for Enzo and Maria to spend a cozy day indoors. After their peaceful walk through the park, their relationship had continued to grow in a way that felt easy and natural. They talked almost every day, and their time together, whether simple or special, was filled with laughter and meaningful conversations. With the world outside blanketed in snow and the temperature dropping to biting lows, they decided to stay in for the day—no plans, no distractions, just the two of them.

It was a lazy Saturday morning when Enzo arrived at Maria's apartment, a bag of groceries in hand. He'd volunteered to cook for her, hoping to make something warm and comforting to match the mood of the day.

"Hey, you're just in time," Maria greeted him with a smile as she opened the door, already dressed in comfortable clothes—an oversized sweater and cozy socks. "Come on in. It's freezing out there."

Enzo stepped inside, the warmth of her apartment immediately wrapping around him. The soft glow of candles flickered from the kitchen counter, and the scent of freshly brewed coffee filled the air. The apartment felt like a sanctuary from the icy world outside, and Enzo was more than ready to settle in for the day.

"Wow, it's so cozy in here," Enzo said as he set the groceries on the counter. "You weren't kidding about making this a stay-in kind of day."

Maria chuckled, tucking a strand of hair behind her ear. "I figured if we're going to spend the day indoors, we might as well go all out. I've got blankets, movies, and all the coffee you could ever need."

Enzo grinned, pulling out the ingredients for their meal. "Sounds perfect. How about I make us something to eat, and then we can hunker down for the day?"

Maria smiled, leaning against the counter as she watched him unpack. "That sounds amazing. What are you making?"

"Something simple, but cozy—homemade chicken soup," Enzo replied, glancing up at her. "I figured it would be perfect for a day like today."

Maria's eyes lit up. "That sounds perfect. You cook, and I'll be your sous-chef."

They worked together in the kitchen, the radio playing softly in the background as they chopped vegetables and stirred the broth. The sound of the bubbling pot filled the room, and the warmth from the stove added to the already inviting atmosphere of Maria's apartment. Enzo loved moments like this—where everything felt easy and unhurried, where he could just enjoy being in Maria's presence without the rush of the outside world.

As they cooked, they talked about their favorite winter memories—snow days as kids, family traditions, and the small joys that came from being inside on cold days like this one. Maria told him about how she used to spend entire days making forts out of blankets and reading books when the weather was too harsh to go outside, and Enzo shared stories of building snowmen with his brother and niece.

The soup was finished before they knew it, and Enzo ladled it into two bowls, carrying them over to the small dining table where Maria had set up a simple but cozy meal. The steam from the soup rose in soft clouds, and the smell of the broth filled the air, making the whole apartment feel even warmer.

"This smells incredible," Maria said as she took a seat, wrapping her hands around the bowl to warm them. "I can't wait to try it."

Enzo smiled, watching as she took her first spoonful. "Well, I hope it lives up to your expectations."

Maria's eyes widened as she tasted the soup, a satisfied smile spreading across her face. "It's perfect. Seriously, Enzo, this is exactly what I needed today."

They ate in comfortable silence for a while, the quiet punctuated only by the soft clink of their spoons against the bowls and the occasional hum of the radio. Outside, the snow continued to fall steadily, creating a beautiful, serene backdrop to their cozy day indoors.

When they finished eating, Maria stood up and stretched. "I don't know about you, but I'm ready for the movie portion of the day. Want to help me build a blanket fort?"

Enzo chuckled, standing up and following her into the living room. "A blanket fort, huh? I haven't done that in years, but I'm game."

Maria grinned, already gathering blankets and pillows from her closet. Together, they transformed her living room into a makeshift fort, draping blankets over the back of the couch and piling pillows underneath to create a comfortable nest. It was simple and playful, and Enzo found himself laughing as they worked, enjoying the carefree nature of it all.

When they finished, they crawled inside, the soft glow of the television casting a warm light over the space. Maria handed him the remote. "You get to pick the first movie."

Enzo took the remote with a grin, scrolling through the options. "Okay, but I warn you, I'm picking something classic. How do you feel about *The Princess Bride*?"

Maria's face lit up. "I love that movie! Excellent choice."

They settled in, the warmth of the blankets and the sound of the movie filling the small space they had created. Enzo felt completely at peace, the simple pleasure of being with Maria making the day feel even more special. There was no need for grand gestures or big plans—just being together like this was enough.

Halfway through the movie, Maria shifted closer to him, resting her head on his shoulder. Enzo glanced down at her, smiling softly as he wrapped his arm around her, pulling her closer. The rhythm of the movie played on in the background, but all Enzo could think about was how right this moment felt—how natural it was to be here with her, sharing this day of quiet comfort.

As the movie ended, neither of them moved, content to stay wrapped in the warmth of the fort they had built. The day had passed by in a blur of simple pleasures, and now, as the afternoon faded into evening, the coziness of the moment deepened.

"I could get used to this," Maria said softly, her voice a little drowsy. "Just spending the day indoors, doing nothing but being lazy and comfortable."

Enzo chuckled, "Same here. It's nice to slow down for a change."

Maria looked up at him, her eyes soft and warm. "I'm really glad you're here, Enzo. I know we've only known each other for a short time, but it feels like we've been doing this forever."

Enzo's heart swelled at her words, and he smiled, brushing a strand of hair away from her face. "I feel the same way. Every moment with you just feels... easy. Like this is exactly where I'm supposed to be."

The day had been perfect in its simplicity—no grand plans, no special occasions—just the two of them, enjoying the warmth of each other's company. And as the evening stretched on, Enzo couldn't help but feel that this was what he had been searching for all along—a relationship built on moments like these, where the quiet was just as meaningful as the laughter.

Together, they watched the snow fall, the world outside their blanket fort fading away as they sank deeper into the cozy comfort of the day.

Chapter 18: New Year's Plans

The holiday season was still alive as the new year was fast approaching. After their cozy day indoors, Enzo and Maria found themselves thinking about the future—about what the next year might hold for them as individuals, and more importantly, as a couple. The easy rhythm they had fallen into over the holidays had been wonderful, but now that the festive season had passed, it was time to start thinking about the bigger picture.

Enzo had been reflecting on the direction his life was taking, not just in terms of his career, but also in the new and exciting relationship he had built with Maria. It was clear that they were both committed to each other, and with the new year just beginning, Enzo felt it was the perfect time for them to sit down and talk about their goals, both individually and together.

It was a Saturday afternoon when they met up at a small café downtown, the sun shining through the windows, casting soft light across the wooden tables. The snow from earlier in the week had started to melt, giving the city a crisp, fresh look as it slowly transitioned from winter into the new year.

Maria arrived first, already seated at a corner table with two steaming mugs of coffee when Enzo walked in. She smiled as he approached, and Enzo couldn't help but feel a rush of warmth at the sight of her. Even after the holiday rush, their connection felt as strong as ever.

"Hey," Enzo said, sliding into the seat across from her. "Thanks for grabbing the coffee."

"Of course," Maria replied, her eyes twinkling. "I figured we could use it. Plus, I wanted to get here early and have a moment to think."

Enzo raised an eyebrow. "A moment to think? That sounds serious."

Maria chuckled softly, shaking her head. "Not serious, but... I guess I've just been thinking a lot about the new year. About us, about where we're headed."

Enzo nodded, understanding immediately. He had been thinking about the same thing. "Yeah, me too. I figured now that the holidays are over, it's a good time to talk about what's next for us."

Maria sipped her coffee, her eyes searching his. "Exactly. I feel like everything moved so quickly during the holidays, and while it was amazing, now that things are slowing down, I want to make sure we're on the same page."

Enzo leaned back in his chair, taking a moment to gather his thoughts. "I'm really glad you brought that up, because I've been feeling the same way. The holidays were incredible—everything with you has been incredible—but I don't want it to feel like things are just fizzling out now that the new year is here. I want to make plans together."

Maria smiled, visibly relieved that they were both on the same wavelength. "I feel the same way. It's not just about how great the holidays were; it's about what comes next. I want us to keep building something, to look forward to the future together."

Enzo nodded, feeling a sense of excitement at the idea of making plans with Maria. "So, what are you thinking? What do you want for the new year—for us?"

Maria took a deep breath, her fingers lightly tracing the rim of her coffee cup as she thought. "Well, for one thing, I want to make sure we keep spending time together, even when life gets busy. I know the holidays gave us a lot of free time, but once work and everything else picks up again, I want to make sure we don't lose that."

"I couldn't agree more," Enzo said. "I've been thinking about that too. I want to prioritize us, no matter how busy things get. We should plan things—dates, trips, whatever it takes to make sure we stay connected."

Maria's eyes lit up at the mention of trips. "I love that idea. I've been wanting to travel more, and I think it would be amazing if we could plan something together this year. Maybe a weekend getaway or even something bigger."

Enzo smiled, already imagining the possibilities. "A getaway sounds perfect. Maybe somewhere quiet, where we can just relax and spend time together. I've been meaning to do more hiking, and I know you've mentioned you enjoy the outdoors."

Maria grinned, clearly excited at the prospect. "That sounds perfect. I'd love to do something like that."

They continued talking, their conversation flowing easily as they discussed the places they wanted to visit, the things they wanted to do together, and how they planned to stay connected throughout the year. It was clear that they were both committed to building something lasting—something that went beyond the holiday magic and into the everyday moments of life.

After a while, Maria's expression grew a little more serious, and she glanced down at her coffee cup before speaking. "There's something else I've been thinking about too," she said softly. "I don't want to put any pressure on us, but... what are we? I mean, where do you see this going?"

Enzo paused, realizing that this was the heart of the conversation they needed to have. He had been thinking about it too, and while they had shared so much already, they hadn't really defined what their relationship was.

"I'm glad you brought that up," Enzo said carefully, his tone sincere. "Because I've been thinking about it too. Maria, I know things have moved fast, and I don't want to rush anything, but I also don't want to pretend like this isn't real. What I feel for you—it's not just a holiday fling. I'm serious about you."

Maria looked up at him, her eyes soft but full of emotion. "I feel the same way, Enzo. This has been the most meaningful connection I've had in a long time. I want to take it seriously too."

Enzo reached across the table, taking her hand in his. "So, let's not complicate it. We're together, and we'll figure out the rest as we go. I'm committed to this—to you."

Maria smiled, a sense of relief and happiness washing over her face. "I like the sound of that. Together."

They sat in silence for a moment, both of them feeling the weight of the conversation lift as they solidified their plans for the future. It wasn't just about making travel plans or finding time for dates—it was about the commitment they were making to each other, to being present and intentional in their relationship.

"So, any other big plans for the new year?" Maria asked, her tone lighter now that the serious part of the conversation was behind them.

Enzo chuckled, shaking his head. "I think that covers most of it. Although, I wouldn't mind learning how to cook more. You've got me beat in that department."

Maria laughed, playfully nudging his foot under the table. "Well, I guess we'll just have to add cooking lessons to the list."

They spent the rest of the afternoon at the café, sipping their coffee and planning the adventures they would have together in the coming year. The excitement of the unknown didn't feel daunting anymore—instead, it felt like an opportunity to build something even more meaningful with each passing day.

Chapter 19: A Snowy Getaway

Enzo and Maria's commitment to planning more time together had already led them to their first adventure as a couple: a weekend getaway to a quiet cabin in the mountains. With both of them loving the outdoors, they had decided to take a trip to enjoy the snow, the serene beauty of nature, and the peacefulness that came with escaping the city.

Enzo had found a cozy, secluded cabin nestled deep in the woods, surrounded by tall pine trees and blanketed in fresh snow. The idea of spending a few days there, away from work, away from distractions, filled him with anticipation. This getaway would be their first trip together, and he wanted everything to be perfect.

Maria had been just as excited about the idea, especially when Enzo had mentioned the nearby hiking trails and the possibility of snowshoeing. It was the kind of trip that felt made for them—a blend of adventure and relaxation, with plenty of time to just enjoy each other's company.

They set out early on a Friday morning, the car packed with warm clothes, snacks, and supplies for their stay. The drive to the cabin took them out of the city and into the rolling hills, where the roads began to twist and wind through snow-covered forests. The landscape changed as they climbed higher into the mountains, the snow getting thicker, the air crisper, and the world around them growing quieter.

"This is going to be amazing," Maria said from the passenger seat, her excitement palpable. She had her phone out, snapping pictures of the snow-covered trees as they passed. "I can't remember the last time I've been somewhere this peaceful."

Enzo smiled, keeping his eyes on the road but feeling the same excitement. "I've been looking forward to this for days. Just us, the snow, and nothing else to worry about."

It didn't take long for them to reach the cabin. As they pulled up the gravel driveway, the sight of the small wooden house nestled against the trees took Enzo's breath away. The cabin was surrounded by a blanket of untouched snow, its chimney already puffing a thin trail of smoke into the clear blue sky. It looked like something out of a postcard, perfectly picturesque and inviting.

Maria practically bounced in her seat as she unbuckled her seatbelt. "This is beautiful! It's even better than I imagined."

Enzo chuckled, opening the car door and stepping out into the crisp mountain air. The silence of the forest enveloped them immediately, broken only by the soft crunch of their boots in the snow as they made their way to the cabin door. Enzo unlocked it and pushed it open, revealing the warm, cozy interior—a living room with a stone fireplace, soft rugs, and a large bay window that looked out onto the snowy landscape.

Maria stepped inside, her eyes wide with appreciation. "This is perfect, Enzo."

He smiled, feeling proud that everything had come together so well. "I'm glad you like it. It's going to be a great weekend."

They quickly unpacked and settled in, lighting a fire in the fireplace and changing into their warmest clothes. Enzo had planned for them to spend part of the day exploring the area, maybe even snowshoeing on one of the nearby trails. But first, they sat down by the fire, sipping hot chocolate and just enjoying the quiet.

"This is exactly what I needed," Maria said softly, leaning back against the couch with a contented sigh. "No noise, no stress, just peace."

Enzo nodded, gazing into the crackling flames. "Same here. I feel like we've both been running nonstop for the past few weeks. This is the perfect way to reset."

After an hour or so of relaxing, they decided to head out for their first adventure of the trip. Enzo had rented snowshoes for them, and they bundled up in their coats, hats, and gloves before heading out into the snowy woods. The snow crunched beneath their feet as they walked, the sun shining brightly overhead, casting long shadows on the snow.

The air was cold, but not uncomfortably so, and the silence of the forest made the whole experience feel almost magical. The only sounds were the rhythmic crunch of their snowshoes and the occasional chirp of a bird from high in the trees.

Maria walked beside him, her cheeks flushed from the cold, her eyes bright with wonder. "This is incredible. I can't believe how quiet it is out here."

Enzo smiled, his breath visible in the air. "It's amazing, isn't it? It's like the whole world has paused."

They followed a trail that wound through the woods, eventually leading them to a small frozen pond. The surface of the ice reflected the sky above, and the snow-covered trees stood like silent sentinels around it, their branches heavy with snow.

"Wow," Maria whispered, stopping at the edge of the pond. "It's beautiful."

Enzo nodded, taking in the serene beauty of the scene. "It really is. It's moments like this that make me feel so lucky."

Maria glanced at him, her smile soft and warm. "Lucky to be here, or lucky to be with me?"

Enzo grinned, stepping closer to her. "Both."

She laughed softly, reaching out to take his hand. They stood there for a moment, just taking it all in—the silence of the forest, the beauty of the snow, and the feeling of being completely in the moment together.

As they walked back to the cabin, the conversation flowed easily between them, the bond they shared deepening with each step. Enzo felt a sense of peace settle over him—like the worries of the world had melted away, leaving only this quiet, perfect moment.

That evening, back at the cabin, they cooked dinner together, enjoying the warmth of the fire as the snow continued to fall softly outside. The cozy atmosphere of the cabin, combined with the simplicity of the day, made everything feel effortless. They talked about their plans for the future, the trips they wanted to take, and the adventures they still had ahead of them.

Later, as they sat by the fire, wrapped in blankets and sipping wine, Enzo felt a sense of contentment he hadn't experienced in a long time. The simplicity of the day—the snow, the quiet, the laughter they had shared—made him realize just how much he valued moments like these.

"I'm really glad we did this," Maria said softly, her head resting on Enzo's shoulder. "It's exactly what I needed to start the year off right."

Enzo smiled, "Me too. This weekend has been perfect."

They stayed like that for a while, the warmth of the fire casting a soft glow over the room, the sound of the snow falling outside creating a peaceful backdrop. It was one of those moments that felt timeless, where everything in the world seemed to align perfectly.

Chapter 20: The First Kiss

Enzo couldn't remember a day that felt more perfect than the one he had just spent with Maria during their snowy getaway. The peacefulness of the mountains, the adventure of exploring the trails, and the cozy warmth of the cabin had made everything feel magical. But now, as they sat together in front of the crackling fire, the moment felt even more significant. It was as if the world had quietly conspired to bring them to this exact point—where something important, something unforgettable, was about to happen.

After their long day of hiking and exploring, the two of them were wrapped up in blankets on the couch, their legs stretched out in front of the fire. Maria leaned comfortably against Enzo's shoulder, her presence a comforting warmth in the room. The snow outside had picked up again, swirling softly past the windows, and the glow of the fire cast a golden light across the cabin.

For a while, neither of them spoke, content to simply be in each other's company. The stillness of the moment felt intimate, like a pause before something important was about to begin.

Maria sighed softly, her voice quiet when she finally spoke. "Today was incredible. I can't remember the last time I felt this... peaceful."

Enzo smiled, feeling her words echo his own thoughts. "Same here. I feel like we're in our own little world up here. It's perfect."

Maria looked up at him, her eyes soft and filled with a kind of tenderness that made Enzo's heart skip a beat. "I've been thinking a lot lately," she said, her voice barely above a whisper. "About us. About how everything has happened so fast, but it feels... right."

Enzo's heart raced as he listened to her words, feeling the weight of what she was saying. He had been thinking the same thing. There was something undeniable between them—something that had been building since the moment they met. The holidays had brought them together quickly, but now, as they sat here, the connection between them felt deeper, more real.

"I've been thinking about that too," Enzo said softly, turning to face her fully. "Everything with you feels... different. But in the best way. Like it was always meant to happen."

Maria smiled, her eyes shining in the firelight. "I didn't expect any of this when we met, but now I can't imagine it any other way. You've made this holiday season more special than I ever thought it could be."

Enzo felt his chest tighten with emotion. The vulnerability in her words, the way she looked at him, made him feel like this moment—this quiet, perfect moment—was leading them toward something inevitable.

For a long moment, they simply looked at each other, the fire crackling softly in the background, the world outside falling away. The weight of everything they had shared, from their first meeting to the snowball fight, to the family dinners and their intimate conversations, hung in the air between them.

And then, slowly, almost instinctively, Enzo leaned in.

His heart raced as he closed the distance between them, his eyes searching Maria's for any sign of hesitation. But there was none. Instead, there was a softness, a quiet anticipation that made Enzo's breath catch in his throat.

Their lips met in a soft, tender kiss, the warmth of it melting away any lingering uncertainty. It was gentle at first, a simple expression of the connection they had felt growing for weeks, but it quickly deepened. The feel of Maria's lips against his, the warmth of her body pressed close to him, sent a surge of emotion through Enzo that he hadn't expected.

This kiss wasn't just about the moment—it was about everything that had come before it. Every laugh they had shared, every quiet conversation, every look that had passed between them, all led to this.

It was the culmination of the closeness they had built, the bond that had formed so naturally between them.

When they finally pulled apart, their foreheads resting gently against each other, Enzo could see the same emotion reflected in Maria's eyes. Her breath was warm against his skin, her smile soft and full of meaning.

"That," she whispered, her voice filled with quiet awe, "was perfect."

Enzo smiled, his heart still racing. "It really was."

They sat there for a moment longer, wrapped in the warmth of the fire and the intimacy of the moment, neither of them wanting to break the spell that had settled over them. The first kiss had felt like more than just a physical connection—it had felt like the start of something deeper, something real.

"I've been wanting to do that for a while," Enzo admitted softly, his voice low.

Maria laughed quietly, her fingers lightly tracing the edge of his jaw. "Me too. I was just waiting for the right moment."

"Well," Enzo said, grinning, "I think we found it."

Maria smiled, her eyes sparkling with warmth. "I think so too."

They kissed again, this time with more certainty, more confidence in what they had together. The warmth between them grew, and Enzo felt a sense of contentment wash over him. This was where he was meant to be—right here, with Maria, in this cabin, with the snow falling gently outside and the fire crackling beside them.

As the night wore on, they stayed wrapped up together, sharing stories, laughter, and more kisses as the fire slowly died down. The connection between them felt stronger than ever, like they had crossed a threshold into something new, something lasting.

Eventually, as the fire flickered its last, they curled up together under the blankets, Maria's head resting on Enzo's chest. The quiet of the cabin, the soft glow of the embers, and the warmth of their closeness made the world outside feel distant, almost unreal.

Enzo pressed a soft kiss to the top of Maria's head, his heart full. He knew that this wasn't just a fleeting moment of holiday magic—this was something real, something that would last long after the snow melted and the lights were taken down.

Chapter 21: New Year's Eve Magic

The days leading up to New Year's Eve seemed to pass in a blur for Enzo and Maria, filled with the warmth of their deepening connection and the memories of their snowy getaway. But now, as New Year's Eve approached, they both felt a quiet anticipation, knowing that the holiday season was about to come to a close and the new year would bring new beginnings. They had made plans to spend the evening together, celebrating not only the end of the year but also everything they had shared during these past few magical weeks.

Enzo arrived at Maria's apartment just as the sky was beginning to darken, the last traces of sunlight fading into the horizon. The city was alive with the excitement of New Year's Eve—people bustling about, fireworks vendors setting up in the distance, and the air filled with a sense of celebration. But for Enzo, the only thing he was looking forward to was spending the night with Maria.

He knocked on the door, and when Maria opened it, his breath caught. She was wearing a simple, elegant dress that shimmered softly in the light, her hair falling in loose waves over her shoulders. Her eyes sparkled as she smiled at him, and Enzo couldn't help but feel like the luckiest man in the world.

"Wow," he said, his voice full of admiration. "You look stunning."

Maria blushed, her smile widening. "Thank you. You don't look so bad yourself."

Enzo had opted for a classic look—dark slacks, a crisp white shirt, and a well-tailored jacket. He'd wanted to make the evening special, and seeing the way Maria looked at him, he knew he'd made the right choice.

"Ready for a magical night?" Maria asked as she stepped aside to let him in.

"More than ready," Enzo replied, stepping inside and taking her hand. "I've been looking forward to this all week."

Maria had planned a quiet evening for the two of them, starting with a candlelit dinner at her apartment before heading out to watch the fireworks at midnight. She had gone all out—preparing a delicious meal, setting the table with soft, flickering candles, and decorating the space with twinkling lights that made the apartment feel like a winter wonderland.

As they sat down to dinner, the conversation flowed easily, the comfort of their growing relationship evident in every shared glance and laugh. They talked about their favorite moments from the past year, the adventures they had planned for the next, and the simple joy of being able to ring in the new year together.

"This has been the best holiday season I've ever had," Maria said softly as they finished their meal. "And I think it's because of you."

Enzo felt a surge of warmth at her words. "I feel the same way. I didn't know what to expect when we first met, but now... I can't imagine it any other way."

Maria smiled, her eyes soft and full of emotion. "I think this is just the beginning, Enzo. There's so much more ahead of us."

Enzo reached across the table, taking her hand in his. "I couldn't agree more. I'm excited to see what the new year brings—for both of us."

After dinner, they bundled up in their coats and scarves and headed out into the night, hand in hand. The streets were alive with people celebrating, the excitement of the approaching midnight hour palpable in the air. Enzo and Maria made their way to a nearby park where the city was hosting a fireworks display. The park had been transformed into a festive gathering place, with twinkling lights wrapped around the trees and small bonfires scattered throughout for warmth.

They found a spot near the edge of the crowd, the perfect vantage point for watching the fireworks. The air was crisp and cold, but the warmth between them made everything feel perfect. Maria leaned into

Enzo, her head resting on his shoulder as they waited for the countdown to midnight.

"This is magical," Maria whispered, looking up at the sky. "There's something about New Year's Eve that feels so... full of possibility."

Enzo smiled, his arm wrapped around her waist. "I know what you mean. It's like everything resets, and we get a fresh start."

The minutes ticked by, the crowd growing more excited as the countdown to midnight approached. Enzo could feel his heart racing, not just because of the fireworks or the celebration, but because of Maria—because of everything they had shared and everything that was still to come. This moment felt important, like a turning point in their relationship, and he wanted to make sure it was as special as it felt.

As the final minute approached, the crowd began to count down, the excitement building with each number. Enzo turned to Maria, his heart pounding as the seconds ticked away.

"Maria," he said softly, his voice barely audible over the crowd. "I'm so glad I met you. This has been the best holiday season of my life, and it's because of you. I can't wait to see what the new year brings for us."

Maria's eyes filled with emotion, and she smiled up at him, her voice just as quiet. "Me too, Enzo. This is just the beginning."

The crowd reached the final seconds of the countdown, the energy buzzing in the air around them. Enzo looked into Maria's eyes, his heart full as the final number was shouted:

"Three... two... one!"

Fireworks exploded overhead, lighting up the sky in brilliant bursts of color and light. The crowd cheered, the sounds of celebration filling the air, but for Enzo, the only thing that mattered in that moment was Maria. He leaned in, capturing her lips in a soft, lingering kiss as the fireworks sparkled above them.

The kiss felt like everything they had shared—the laughter, the quiet moments, the adventures—had led them to this exact point. It was a promise, an unspoken understanding that whatever the new year held, they would face it together.

When they finally pulled apart, the sky was still ablaze with fireworks, but Maria's eyes were locked on his, filled with a warmth that made Enzo's heart swell.

"Happy New Year, Enzo," she whispered, her voice full of emotion.

"Happy New Year, Maria," Enzo replied, his voice soft and full of meaning.

They stood there for a moment longer, watching the fireworks as they lit up the night sky, their arms wrapped around each other. The magic of the moment wasn't just in the fireworks or the celebration—it was in the connection they had built, the bond that had grown stronger with every passing day.

Chapter 22: The Midnight Moment

The new year had arrived, bringing with it a sense of excitement and possibility for Enzo and Maria. After their magical New Year's Eve celebration, they had fallen into a comfortable routine—spending more time together, sharing dreams and plans for the year ahead, and growing even closer. But there was one moment from that night that stood out to Enzo—the midnight moment when they had kissed under the fireworks.

It wasn't just the kiss itself, though it had been perfect. It was the way the world had seemed to pause, the way everything had felt so right. Enzo couldn't shake the feeling that something important had shifted between them in that moment, and now, as they entered the first days of the new year, he found himself thinking about it more and more.

Maria had invited him over for a quiet evening at her apartment, a chance to relax after the excitement of the holidays. The world outside had returned to its usual pace, but for Enzo, time still felt slower when he was with Maria, like every moment with her was something to savor.

When he arrived, the apartment was warm and inviting, the soft glow of lamps casting a cozy light across the room. Maria had changed into comfortable clothes—a simple sweater and leggings—and Enzo felt an immediate sense of ease wash over him as he stepped inside.

"Hey," Maria greeted him with a smile, stepping forward to give him a quick kiss on the cheek. "I'm glad you're here. I've been looking forward to tonight."

Enzo smiled, feeling the same warmth he always felt around her. "Me too. It's nice to slow down after everything."

They settled in on the couch, a blanket draped over their laps as they sipped glasses of wine and caught up on how the first few days of the new year had been treating them. The conversation flowed easily, as it always did, but there was something on Enzo's mind—something he had been thinking about since their kiss on New Year's Eve.

After a while, Maria leaned her head on his shoulder, the comfort of the moment wrapping around them like a cocoon. "I've been thinking a lot about New Year's Eve," she said softly, her voice barely above a whisper. "About the kiss... about that moment. It felt so... important."

Enzo's heart skipped a beat. He hadn't expected her to bring it up, but hearing her say it made him realize that she had felt the same way he had.

"I've been thinking about it too," Enzo admitted, turning to look at her. "It wasn't just a kiss, was it? It felt like more than that. Like something changed between us."

Maria lifted her head, her eyes meeting his with the same intensity he had felt during their midnight moment. "Exactly. It was like everything we've been building, everything we've been feeling, came together in that moment. And I think... I think it's because we both know this is real. That this is something we want to last."

Enzo nodded, his heart full as he listened to her words. "I feel the same way, Maria. Everything with you has felt different from the start—like it was meant to happen. And when we kissed at midnight, it felt like a promise. That whatever comes next, we'll face it together."

Maria smiled, her eyes soft and full of emotion. "I like the sound of that. A promise."

They sat in silence for a moment, the weight of their words settling between them. The kiss had been more than just a physical connection—it had been a turning point in their relationship, a moment of clarity where they both realized just how much they meant to each other.

Enzo took a deep breath, knowing there was something else he wanted to say—something he had been feeling for a while but hadn't had the courage to admit until now.

"Maria," he said quietly, his voice steady but full of emotion, "I think I'm falling in love with you."

Maria's eyes widened slightly, her breath catching in her throat. For a moment, she didn't say anything, and Enzo wondered if he had said too much, if he had spoken too soon. But then, a smile spread across her face, and she reached out to take his hand.

"I think I'm falling in love with you too, Enzo," she whispered, her voice filled with quiet certainty. "I've been feeling it for a while, but I didn't want to rush things. But now... I know it's real. I love how easy everything feels with you, how natural it is to be together."

Enzo's heart swelled with emotion. Hearing those words from her made everything feel even more real. This wasn't just a holiday romance, something that would fade once the excitement of the season was over. This was love—something that was growing stronger every day.

He pulled her closer, pressing a soft kiss to her forehead. "I'm so glad you feel the same way. I didn't know what to expect when we first met, but now... I can't imagine my life without you."

Maria smiled, her eyes shining with emotion. "Me either. I didn't expect this at all, but it feels like exactly where we're supposed to be."

They kissed again, this time with more certainty, more understanding of what they were building together. The kiss wasn't about the fireworks or the magic of the holidays—it was about the love that had grown between them, the bond that had deepened with every shared moment.

As they pulled apart, Maria leaned her head back on Enzo's shoulder, her voice soft and full of contentment. "That midnight moment was when I knew," she whispered. "When I knew I was falling in love with you."

Enzo smiled, his heart full. "Same here. I think that moment changed everything."

Chapter 23: The Vow

As winter began to loosen its grip and the new year settled into a steady rhythm, Enzo and Maria found themselves more connected than ever. Their relationship had grown stronger with each passing day, built on the solid foundation they had laid during the holidays. They had shared laughter, adventure, quiet moments, and, most importantly, the kind of love that felt like it would last a lifetime.

It had been a few months since their first kiss under the New Year's Eve fireworks, and everything between them felt effortless. They spent their weekends exploring the city, enjoying quiet dinners, and planning for future trips. But there was something about their connection—something deeper—that made each moment together feel significant, like they were on the brink of something even more meaningful.

One day, after a long afternoon spent hiking one of their favorite trails, Enzo suggested something that had been on his mind for a while: a trip back to the park where they had first met, the mall where their story had started. He wanted to return to that moment, to revisit the place where their love had begun, but this time with a different purpose.

Maria agreed enthusiastically, her eyes bright with excitement at the idea of revisiting the place where they had shared so many important moments. They planned the trip for the following weekend, both of them eager to relive the memories of that fateful Christmas Eve when their paths had crossed.

When the day arrived, the air was crisp but not as cold as it had been that winter. The snow had melted, giving way to the first signs of spring, but the city was still dotted with remnants of the holiday decorations. Enzo and Maria made their way to the mall, hand in hand, their hearts light with anticipation.

As they stepped inside the familiar building, Enzo couldn't help but smile. The last time they had been here, it had been filled with the hustle and bustle of Christmas shoppers, the air electric with holiday excitement. Now, the mall was quieter, but for Enzo, it was no less significant. This place had become a symbol of everything that had brought them together.

They wandered through the stores, laughing and reminiscing about their first meeting—the way they had reached for the same toy at the exact same moment, the way their eyes had met and something unspoken had passed between them. It had been the start of something unexpected but beautiful, and now, standing here with Maria, Enzo knew that moment had changed his life forever.

After a while, they made their way to the park outside the mall, the place where they had shared their first real conversation. The park looked different now, with the snow gone and the trees beginning to bloom with the first signs of spring. But the memories of that night, of their midnight stroll and the warmth they had shared, lingered in the air.

They walked to the spot where they had sat on that first night, near the small fountain in the center of the park. Enzo could feel his heart racing, not from nerves, but from the overwhelming feeling of love and certainty that had been growing inside him for months.

"Do you remember this spot?" Enzo asked softly as they sat down on the bench, their hands still intertwined.

Maria smiled, her eyes sparkling with the same warmth they had held that night. "Of course I do. This is where everything really began for us."

Enzo nodded, his heart full. "That night changed everything for me, Maria. I didn't know it at the time, but meeting you... it was the start of something I'd been searching for, even if I didn't realize it. And now, looking back, I can't imagine my life without you."

Maria's eyes softened, and she squeezed his hand gently. "I feel the same way. Meeting you was the best thing that's ever happened to me."

Enzo took a deep breath, knowing that the moment had come. He reached into his pocket, his fingers closing around the small velvet box he had been carrying with him for days. This was it—the vow he had been waiting to make.

"Maria," he began, his voice steady but filled with emotion, "we've been through so much together already. From that first moment we met to everything we've shared since then, you've shown me what real love feels like. You've made me laugh, you've made me feel understood, and you've made me want to be the best version of myself. And now, I want to spend the rest of my life showing you how much you mean to me."

Maria's eyes widened, her breath catching as she realized what was happening.

Enzo dropped to one knee in front of her, opening the small box to reveal a simple but elegant ring. His heart was pounding, but his voice was calm, full of love and certainty.

"Maria, will you marry me?"

Tears filled Maria's eyes as she looked down at him, her hand covering her mouth in surprise. For a moment, neither of them spoke, the world around them seeming to pause as the weight of the moment settled between them.

And then, with a radiant smile, Maria nodded, her voice barely above a whisper. "Yes. Yes, Enzo. I will."

Enzo's heart soared as he slipped the ring onto her finger, standing up to pull her into a tight embrace. The joy and love between them felt overwhelming, like everything they had built, everything they had shared, had led them to this exact moment.

They kissed, the warmth of the vow they had just made filling the air around them. It wasn't just a promise for the future—it was a commitment to everything they had already shared, to the love that had grown between them since that first fateful meeting.

As they stood together in the park, the spring breeze gently brushing past them, Enzo knew that this was only the beginning. The holidays, the adventures, the laughter—it had all led to this moment. And now, as they prepared to face the future together, Enzo felt a sense of peace, knowing that whatever came next, they would face it with love, with trust, and with the unbreakable bond they had built.

Maria looked up at him, her eyes shining with love. "This is the best day of my life," she whispered, her voice full of emotion.

Enzo smiled, his heart full. "Mine too. And I promise, every day after this will be just as beautiful."

With the vow made, they walked out of the park, hand in hand, ready to face whatever the future held for them. Their love had started with a chance meeting, but now it was a love that would last a lifetime—one built on trust, on laughter, and on the promise they had made to each other.

Enzo and Maria walked into their future, together, with a vow that would never be broken.

Milton Keynes UK
Ingram Content Group UK Ltd.
UKHW032035191024
449814UK00010B/519

9 798227 843753